A CANDLELIGHT ROMANCE

CANDLELIGHT ROMANCES

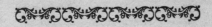

Hibiscus Lagoon

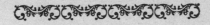

Dorothy Dowdell

A CANDLELIGHT ROMANCE

Published by
Dell Publishing Co., Inc.
1 Dag Hammarskjold Plaza
New York, New York 10017

Dell ® TM 681510, Dell Publishing Co., Inc.

ISBN: 0-440-14494-9

Printed in the United States of America
First printing—February 1981

CHAPTER 1

From her window seat on the huge jet Thayer Elwood looked down at the cloud cover, meringue-thick in spots and then thinning to reveal the Pacific stirred by trade winds to long shallow waves. This was the last leg of her journey from Minneapolis to Pago Pago in American Samoa.

As Thayer unfastened the seat belt from around her slender waist, she tried to ignore the persistent feeling of uneasiness. She pushed a strand of blue-black hair from her face and settled herself for the five-and-a-half-hour flight from Hawaii to Pago Pago.

It wasn't that she was afraid of flying. As a matter of fact she loved it. Since the huge jetliner crossed the ocean constantly, there was no reason to believe other than that they would have a safe flight this time. No, it wasn't fear that nagged her; perhaps it was worry over what lay ahead.

Yet her common sense told her that there was no reason for such anxiety. She was going to work for her father's only brother, though it was true that she'd seldom seen him because of the long distance between Minnesota and Samoa. But her mind went back to the last time he'd returned to Minneapolis for her father's funeral eight months ago. He'd looked and acted so much like her adored father, and had been such a comfort in her numbing grief that she had warmed to him instantly.

After the funeral, when Wilbur Elwood had learned that she was majoring in floriculture at the university, he'd said, "When you graduate, Thayer, come to Samoa and we'll raise orchids to export. It's a big business nowadays. Just let me know when you're ready."

She was a trained floriculturist with a new diploma in her suitcase to prove it, so surely she could handle the orchid-growing project her uncle was establishing on his plantation. So what was her problem? Perhaps it was the puzzling letter she had received from him just a month ago. She opened her purse, which contained the letter, and pulled it out.

But before she had a chance to read it again, a stewardess pushed a cart of assorted drinks down the aisle. Thayer asked for a cup of coffee, and as she sipped it she looked down at the sea again and watched the billows roll and stretch endlessly on all sides. There wasn't a ship or an island to be seen on the vast expanse of water. It was as lonely and empty as a desert.

She stirred worriedly in her seat, trying to assure herself that it was silly to be so uptight. Uncle Wilbur was probably somewhat of a character, (at least that was the impression she got from his letter) but he was a darling too, so much like her father; it would almost be like having him back again. Perhaps she was having a reaction to the fact that she was making a change in her life. There'd been too many changes lately; so many that she felt disoriented and insecure.

First there'd been her father's unexpected death from a cerebral hemorrhage. Even now, as she thought about him, the tears welled in her eyes, for their relationship, based on complete understanding and devotion, had been so close. All of her life her father had told her, "You're a beauty, Thayer. Just like your mother. It's a good thing you look like her and not me." Perhaps she did resemble her mother, but in every other way she took after her father.

It was true that her father wasn't exactly good-

6

looking; his mouth was too big, but it was so quick to smile; his kindly eyes looked out from under eyebrows that were perhaps too heavy; his nose had almost a Roman curve but it was noble. He had strength of character, high ideals and was completely trustworthy. As the minister had said at the funeral, "Richard Elwood was a thoroughly good man."

Thayer had hardly begun to accept his death and conquer her devastating grief when her mother announced that she was going to marry again. Almost too shocked to believe her ears, she'd objected angrily, "How can you, Mother? How can you be so unfeeling? It's only been three months since Daddy died!"

Her mother had tossed back her beautiful dark hair as she shoved her hands into the pockets of her white pantsuit and looked at her defiantly. "It might surprise you to learn that I was once engaged to Tom Ransdell. We were going to be married as soon as I finished college. Then we quarreled and he married someone else. Later I met your father, and you know the rest. But I've always loved Tom and he never forgot me. Now he's divorced and we're going to be married."

How could her mother love another man when she had been lucky enough to be married to her father, one of the finest men on earth? It seemed incredible to Thayer that her mother would even admit to such disloyalty. But then she and her mother had never really understood each other; they had loved each other of course, but it wasn't the same relationship—the same compassion and accord that she had had with her father.

Fury boiled in Thayer as she lashed out at her mother. There had been a bitter quarrel, but her mother had married her mining engineer anyway and gone to live in a remote town in Colorado near a big copper mine. So far her mother hadn't written; even when Thayer graduated from the university, there was no answer to her invitation to attend the ceremonies, nor a gift in acknowledgment. Deeply hurt, she felt she had lost both of her parents.

She turned to Uncle Wilbur, for he was the only close relative she had now. It had taken the very last of her college fund and money she had earned to buy her plane ticket to Samoa, but she would soon be with him and her worries would be over. Wilbur would be like a father to her. They would make a home together and establish their orchid-growing business. This would be a new beginning for them both, and she could put aside her sorrow over losing her parents.

If only her uncle hadn't written that puzzling letter. She finished the last of her coffee, put her cup on the seat tray in front of her, and then took the letter out of the envelope.

Dear Thayer,

I am here at the Samoan Inn in Pago Pago where we will stay for a night or two after you arrive, before we leave for Nanotuma and my plantation. I can hardly wait for you to come because I need your help.

I've been here in Pago Pago seeing my lawyer, Don Alo. I've made out a new will leaving my estate to you. But the main reason I'm here is to get advice on how to fight my neighbor, Eiland von Kuhrt. He's trying to get everything away from me. He's nothing but a thief and he's trying to get my plantation, my workers, and my equipment. But you and I will fight him to the last ditch. He thinks he's the all-powerful King of the Universe who can get by with anything. But you and I will show him, won't we, girl? See you soon.

Wilbur Elwood

She tapped the letter against her teeth. What did her uncle mean that his neighbor was trying to get everything away from him? How could Von Kuhrt do that? And how could she help her uncle "fight him to the last ditch"? Apparently Wilbur intended to take this neighbor to court. But she had no knowledge of the law, so how could she help?

Certainly she couldn't help financially. She smiled ruefully as she thought of the sixty dollars she had in traveler's checks and less than twenty in cash. To help earn the money for her airfare she had given up her room in the campus dormitory the last month and had moved in with an elderly woman who needed care after an operation. But Wilbur was a wealthy planter so money would not be the problem; no doubt he meant that she would give him moral support, but how she dreaded being involved in a neighborhood fight.

She thought of when she had heard the name Von Kuhrt before and remembered that Uncle Wilbur had spoken of a neighbor Gunther von Kuhrt when he had visited in Minneapolis several years ago, but who was this Eiland von Kuhrt? Well, she would soon find out.

She put the letter back in her purse and took out a paperback book on the South Pacific islands that she had bought in the airline terminal in Honolulu. She flipped through the pages and read again that American Samoa had been an unincorporated territory of the United States since 1900. Volcanoes had formed the mountainous islands that made up the territory. The main island of Tutuila, on which Pago Pago was located, was nineteen miles long and six miles across at the widest spot and was just halfway between Honolulu and Sydney. The islands, including Nanotuma to the northeast where her uncle had his plantation, were all very small, just dots in the massive ocean. Altogether they made up about 76 square miles with a total population of only thirty thousand.

How different it would all seem after living in a city as large as Minneapolis and a country as vast as the United States. She couldn't imagine more of a contrast in climate either, between the tropics and the cold winters of Minnesota. It was frightening to think of leaving everything that was dear and familiar, but it would be a challenge, and perhaps that was what she needed at this time.

The hours passed. There was a movie to watch and an early dinner to eat. Finally the pilot announced that in a few minutes they would be landing at Tafuna Airport out of Pago Pago, the main city and capital of American Samoa.

It was still daylight when she spotted the tiny island, an incredibly lush green dot in the dark blue sea. A mist hung over the heavily forested mountain peaks that rose abruptly from the sea. Innumerable bays and coves cut into the irregular shoreline. As they lost altitude, she could see Pago Pago Bay carved fjordlike into the heart of the island, nearly dividing it in half.

Rushing streams and long waterfalls glistened in the dense rain forest. Fertile valleys lay between the mountain peaks, and along the shore palm trees waved back and forth. It was breathtakingly beautiful, and her excitement pushed aside all of her doubts and anxieties.

The plane skimmed over a series of corrugated roofs and touched down on the runway to the modern air terminal. About twenty passengers disembarked from the big jet, and as they walked toward the main building the heat rose from the tarmac like a smothering blanket. Thayer looked for her uncle among the handsome dark-skinned Samoans in gay shirts and dresses who were waiting behind the wire barrier, but she couldn't see him.

She thought he must be in the terminal, but when she entered the cool air-conditioned building and looked around the waiting room, there was no Uncle Wilbur, and her heart sank leadenly. Nervously she fingered the leather strap of her purse as she tried to convince herself that he had just been delayed and would soon be there. As she walked toward the baggage carousel she was barely aware of the laughing, talking people around her. Finally her suitcases appeared and she retrieved them, carried them to the waiting room, and placed them by a chair, wondering what she should do.

It was growing dark. She considered taking the bus outside to the Samoan Inn, thinking that perhaps Uncle Wilbur was there. Numb with jet lag, she never felt so bewildered and lost in her life. She had taken it for granted that her uncle would meet her and take charge. She watched people leave the waiting room and head for the parking area or climb on the bus. Soon she would have to make up her mind what to do or she would be left alone out here.

Then the outside door opened and a tall attractive young man with striking red hair entered, looked around the waiting room, walked toward her, and said, "Pardon me, are you Miss Elwood?"

"Yes, I am." Almost weak with relief, she asked, "Did my uncle send you?"

"Not exactly, but I have come for you. I have my car outside. Let's sit down; I have something to tell you." He took a wallet out of his pocket, extracted a business card, then leaned toward her, hardly knowing how to begin. "First let me introduce myself." He handed her his card. "I am Russell McLeod, an agricultural adviser on the staff of the territorial government."

Unconsciously Thayer braced herself as she took his business card and read it. As if to postpone hearing anything unpleasant, she asked, "If you are an agricul-

11

tural adviser, you no doubt have gone to Seacrest, my uncle's plantation on the island of Nanotuma?"

The young man looked down at his hands, made a tent of his fingers, and said, "Yes, indeed, many times. Wilbur Elwood and I were good friends."

A ball of dread gathered in the pit of her stomach. "You said 'were good friends.' What do you mean?"

"Wilbur had a heart attack a week ago. He was brought here to the hospital, but he died yesterday afternoon. I can't tell you how sorry I am."

CHAPTER 2

As they drove toward the Samoan Inn through the soft, warm darkness in Russell McLeod's subcompact, Thayer shrank into the corner of her seat, too numb and shocked to grasp the full implication of what had happened.

Russell said, "Some of us tried to get in touch with you when Wilbur entered the hospital. I telephoned to the only number your uncle had, but a girl answered and said you had moved out."

She told him about leaving the dormitory to care for the elderly convalescent. "I wrote Uncle Wilbur about it but perhaps he forgot."

Russell went on, "The services will be held tomorrow at two o'clock. Wilbur made all the arrangements for his funeral some time ago. At least you don't have that ordeal to go through."

"Uncle Wilbur must have told you about my arrival on this flight. It was so good of you to meet me. I can't thank you enough."

"I'll be glad to help in any way I can. I assume that you don't know anyone here in Samoa."

"No one at all." Now that Uncle Wilbur and her father were gone and she was out of touch with her mother, there was no one. It was a devastating thought to realize how utterly alone she was. Well, she was twenty-two years old, completely of age, and it was high time that she be on her own, she told herself with more self-assurance than she felt.

As Russell drove along the dark road, he said, "It's a

shame you came so far to see your uncle only to have him gone when you got here. He was certainly looking forward to your visit. Kept saying that he was going to have a member of his family with him for a change. Poor guy, he always struck me as being sort of a lonely fellow. Guess he never married."

She explained how Wilbur had been divorced years before. Then she thought how strange that her uncle hadn't mentioned that she was coming to work rather than just to visit. Had Wilbur even consulted him about the orchid project? It didn't sound that way, but she was too weary and drained to discuss it now. "Tell me about Uncle Wilbur's plantation."

"Well, Seacrest is quite an extensive holding with crops of bananas, coconuts, and other tropical fruits. Taro as well. At one time Wilbur was one of the biggest planters in Samoa."

"You say, 'at one time.' Does that mean that he wasn't lately?"

He hesitated and said finally, "Seacrest has been somewhat neglected these last few years. Of course Wilbur wasn't so young anymore."

"He wasn't so old, either," Thayer protested. "Only fifty-three. Surely he could have supervised his plantation."

"Perhaps he hadn't been so well these last few years. Guess he's been under a lot of stress too."

Of course he'd been under a lot of stress, Thayer told herself, if a neighbor was stealing everything and trying to get control of his plantation. This Eiland von Kuhrt was even trying to get Wilbur's workers and equipment away from him. No wonder her poor uncle had had a fatal heart attack.

For the first time it struck her that the plantation was hers now. She thought of the letter in her purse and the lines, "I've been here in Pago Pago seeing my lawyer,

14

Don Alo. I've made out a new will leaving my estate to you." It all seemed too unreal to grasp, that Uncle Wilbur was gone and the estate was hers. But now the fight was hers as well. At all costs she must not let this evil neighbor take advantage of Wilbur's death, for this would be just the time he would grab everything.

Soon they arrived at the inn, which was built to look like a native village with murals and artifacts of Samoan life decorating the main lobby. As soon as Russell made sure that her reservations were in order and had arranged to pick her up in time for the funeral, he left. Soon Thayer was in her comfortable room, where she showered and climbed into bed, numb and weary.

The next morning Thayer had breakfast on the terrace that overlooked the shimmering blue bay. She could see a patch of green grass surrounded by golden trumpet bushes heavy with large velvety flowers. A black and yellow butterfly, glimmering like a jewel, flitted from blossom to blossom, sometimes disappearing down the long tubelike throats.

While she was eating, a tall man in his early thirties, with dark brown hair and a trim mustache, was shown to a table near her. She could tell by the deferential manner of the waiter that he was someone well-known and important. Fascinated, she watched him out of the corner of her eye, for not only was he unusually handsome, but his urbane and sophisticated manner was that of a true aristocrat.

Finally he looked up from his menu and his eyes met hers, and for a long moment they looked at each other. Her blood stirred and a faint blush rose to her face, then she looked at the sea again, strangely disturbed. She was unaware how beautiful she looked with her hair a dark fluffy cloud framing her exquisite face, with her well-cut pantsuit the same color as the golden trumpet blossoms that formed a background for her. As she

15

left the dining room she glanced toward the stranger again only to find that he was watching her too. Her heart trip-hammered in spite of herself, for he was the most attractive man she had ever seen.

Back in her room she pushed aside thoughts of the handsome stranger and telephoned Don Alo. She found that he was in his office and could meet with her if she would come at once.

As the taxi drove through Pago Pago she looked out at the low buildings roofed with corrugated iron. The area showed the ravages of the tropical climate, and there was little to attract a tourist in the town in spite of the beauty of the setting.

Don Alo's quarters consisted of a modest suite over a small department store. A pretty brown-skinned girl in a halter top and short flowered skirt sat busily typing in the outer room. The lawyer, an older Samoan in a rumpled light suit, greeted her and pulled a chair near his desk. In spite of the early hour the air was muggy and hot. "You'll feel the cool air from the window air-conditioner here. Until your blood thins, you'll notice the heat here in the tropics. But later it isn't so bad." He smiled. He opened a file and took out a thick folder.

The lawyer glanced through the thick pile of papers in the folder. "Did your uncle ever discuss his affairs with you?"

She shook her head but told him about her uncle's plans to start the orchid project.

Don Alo showed his dismay. "He was in no position to embark on such a plan. None at all. I can't imagine why he ever had you come out here for such a reason!"

She leaned forward. "What do you mean?"

Don Alo pointed to the papers in the folder, then flipped through them. "He was on the verge of bankruptcy! Just look at these promissory notes that he

16

couldn't repay. He was deeply in debt to the bank. You have no idea—"

"I don't understand!" she said urgently. She'd believed that Uncle Wilbur had been a successful planter for years.

"Mr. Elwood established almost unlimited credit during his prosperous years. But lately he's gone through some poor times. Crop failures for one reason or another." The lawyer drummed his fingers on the desk. "One year a hurricane leveled most of his banana trees."

"How awful!"

"There seemed to be one thing after another. However, other planters went through the hard times too, but they pulled themselves out of it and were successful again. Wilbur didn't. For the past five years he went downhill and just plunged deeper and deeper into debt."

Tears swam in Thayer's eyes. What was the truth behind all this?

The lawyer picked up one of the promissory notes. "I can't understand it, Miss Elwood. How could he lose all his business acumen? His expertise?"

"He couldn't," she said, shaking her head. "It's almost as if he had an enemy working against him."

Before she could ask about Eiland von Kuhrt, the attorney looked at her with sympathy in his dark eyes and said, "Your uncle made you his sole heir. I'm sorry but there will be very little estate to inherit. It will take everything he had to settle even part of his debts."

"But what about his land? Surely that must be valuable." There was desperation in her voice.

Don Alo shook his head. "He didn't own any. The land at Seacrest was leased. There is very little privately owned land here. We Samoans have always lived under

17

the *matai* system. It goes way back to the very beginning of our ancestry."

"*Matai* system?"

"That means that all people even remotely related to
each other are considered an extended or collective
family called an *aiga*. You'd probably call it a clan. But
the land communally belongs to the *aiga* or family and
not to individuals. Each family has a *matai* or chief who
is the head of the family and caretaker of the land. Out-
siders can lease our land from a *matai* but they cannot
buy it."

Thayer pointed to the promissory notes. "Then how
can a planter borrow money? What is used as security if
he has no land?"

"His buildings. His equipment. His producing trees.
But mostly his reputation. This was true with Wilbur
Elwood. The bank seriously overextended itself with
him. They are trying to retrieve their money now. But
instead of forcing him into bankruptcy, they are having
someone else manage his plantation so it will become
lucrative again."

"It seems so strange that he would get into such a
spot," Thayer said, knowing in her heart that it was this
Eiland von Kuhrt's doing.

Don Alo shook his head. "I can't understand it all.
I've known him for years. I know how successful he
was at one time."

"Someone else brought it all on. Made things happen
to his crops. Tried to ruin him. An enemy—"

The lawyer sat up in surprise. "Oh, Miss Elwood,
you don't mean that! He had no enemies. No one deliberately tried to ruin him."

"I do mean it. In the last letter I got from Uncle
Wilbur he wrote about a man, Eiland von Kuhrt, who
was taking everything away from him."

Don Alo threw his head back and laughed. "You

couldn't be more mistaken. Eiland von Kuhrt is the wealthiest and most respected planter in the islands. He's a descendant of a German nobleman, Baron Eiland von Kuhrt, who came here in 1850 to establish plantations to ship copra to Germany for the extraction of oil. The Von Kuhrts have been prosperous planters ever since."

"That doesn't mean that the present Von Kuhrt is necessarily honest." Anger welled up in her. She sat up straight and stared at him.

"Believe me, Miss Elwood, you're wrong! The present Eiland von Kuhrt is not only a successful planter, but he's a member of the Samoan Senate; he's on many advisory committees to the governor; he's a bank director—"

"No doubt he's a director of the bank that took over my uncle's plantation. Is he?" Her deep violet eyes snapped with fury.

"As a matter of fact he is, but—"

"And who is managing Seacrest to get it back on its feet?"

The lawyer put his two hands flat on his desk and half rose from his chair. "You don't understand—"

Thayer's mouth tightened. "Answer me, please. Who is managing the plantation?"

"Eiland von Kuhrt himself. You see, his home plantation is on Nanotuma Island. It borders Seacrest. He is managing both operations."

With a look of triumph on her face, Thayer sat back in her chair. "Now don't you think that's rather a strange coincidence! A series of unexplained disasters bring hard times to a formerly prosperous plantation. Still the bank extends more loans."

"But, Miss Elwood—"

"Then one of the directors, who just happens to be my uncle's neighbor, insists on calling in the loans. He

19

suggests that the bank take over the management of the plantation to pay off the debt. Out of the goodness of his heart he offers to manage the property along with his own operation. No doubt he was planning to rip off my uncle, the bank, and everyone else and end up with the whole works in his name!"

"Oh, no! That isn't—"

Thayer ignored his protests. "Well, one thing he didn't count on was me! I'm certainly not going to let him get by with it."

The lawyer put his hand on her arm. "Miss Elwood, I beg you, be very discreet with your accusations. Don't do anything until you are thoroughly informed. Mr. von Kuhrt is too prominent, too highly respected to be libeled. And I warn you, he won't stand for it! Be very careful."

"Don't worry, I'll be careful. Why didn't my uncle sue him? He wrote that he had come to see you."

"I discouraged him. He had no case."

Anger flared in her again. It was no use talking to this lawyer. It was obvious that Von Kuhrt had bought him off.

The lawyer tilted back in his chair again. "After the funeral I suggest that you return to Minnesota. There is nothing for you here. I'll keep you informed about the settlement of the estate."

"I have no intentions of leaving at this time," she said coldly. "Is there any reason why I can't go to Seacrest and stay there for a while?"

The attorney shrugged. "No reason at all, if you want to. Mr. von Kuhrt insisted that your uncle keep his home—which is yours now. The housekeeper and her husband are there so you'd be perfectly safe and comfortable."

"Then that's what I'll do. It will give me a chance to

go through his personal effects and see if there are any family keepsakes."

She vowed that she would go through all of his papers and find out the truth about Seacrest. She'd expose Eiland von Kuhrt's trickery no matter how powerful he was. Her uncle had been cheated out of his plantation, and she was being deprived of her rightful inheritance. She was going to stay and get to the bottom of all this wrongdoing.

Surely Don Alo wasn't the only attorney in Pago Pago. He almost seemed to be a henchman of Von Kuhrt's. But now she was forced to pay attention to the lawyer and go over the documents in the folder that represented her uncle's complex affairs. But as soon as possible she had to find someone else to help her.

CHAPTER 3

By the time their conference ended, Thayer was nearly overcome by the tropical heat, so Don Alo called a cab and she returned to her cool hotel room. She took off her damp, sticky clothes, put on a light robe, and sat cross-legged on top of the bed.

It was then that the full impact of her predicament dawned on her and her heart sank in panic. She was thousands of miles from home, had no friends or relatives here and practically no money. There was no one she could call on for help because nothing on earth would make her appeal to her mother for funds. She'd starve first! She didn't qualify for a credit card of any kind. There was no way she could raise the money to buy a ticket back to Minneapolis. She never felt so alone in her life.

Somehow she must get to Nanotuma to the plantation as soon as possible. At least she wouldn't starve there and she'd have a roof over her head.

She promised herself that she would get the best of Eiland von Kuhrt. She could picture him, heavy-featured, beer-swollen, with cruel eyes; then she thought of her kindly, gentle uncle who'd be no match for such an evil bully. Probably the worry of dealing with Von Kuhrt had broken his health, and a recent confrontation had resulted in the fatal heart attack. She lay on the bed and rested.

Later she showered, then dressed in a dark blue sheath with a soft chiffon scarf and put on white sandals. Carrying her white purse, she went to the registration desk in the lobby.

A middle-aged clerk asked, "May I help you?"

"I want to go to the island of Nanotuma. Can you tell me how to get there from here?"

"There's an interisland launch that goes there twice a week, but it left this morning. There won't be another one for three days."

Her disappointment showed in her face. "Oh, I was hoping to go there later this afternoon!" She fought her panic. How could she stay in this expensive hotel for three more days?

Worriedly she turned away and headed for the coffee shop. How much was her room costing? And three more nights—how could she ever pay the bill? Don Alo had said that the funeral bills would be charged to the estate, but how could she ask him for money for herself? Especially since he'd advised her to return to the United States.

She must have been out of her mind to have started out with only sixty dollars in travelers checks and less than twenty dollars in cash. That was hardly enough for two days on her own.

While she ate toast and drank tea for lunch, the cheapest items on the menu, she tried to find a solution. She couldn't appeal to her mother for money; that was completely out. She thought of her friends in Minnesota, but like herself, they were just out of college and looking for jobs. None of them was in any position to make her a loan. She had some distant relatives in Vermont, but she hardly knew them and couldn't ask them for money.

Once the funeral was over, she'd have to cope with her situation. She'd have to find a cheaper place to stay here in Pago Pago until the launch left for the outer islands again. She never felt so discouraged in her life.

23

At one thirty Russell called for her and drove her to a little church on a knoll overlooking the bay. On the way she told him now she had just missed the interisland launch to Nanotuma and how anxious she was to get there.

The church was a wooden New England style complete with a spire. No doubt designed by the early missionaries, it somehow looked fitting among the surrounding palm trees.

By the time they had seated themselves in the front pew on one side of the center aisle, the hushed church was almost filled. There was a slight stir when a group of distinguished-looking men and women was ushered to the reserved pew across the aisle. Russell whispered, "That's the governor and his party."

In the group was the handsome aristocrat whom she had seen earlier in the hotel; he took the seat next to the aisle just a few feet from her. She looked at him, their gaze met and once again she felt an irresistible response to his magnetism. Confused, annoyed with herself, she looked away, the color rising in her neck. Then she couldn't help herself and glanced at him again. He was still looking at her, interest and faint amusement intermingling in the expression around his mouth and in his eyes.

When the service began, all thoughts of the interesting stranger left her and she listened to the Samoan choir sing "Rock of Ages." Tears swam in her eyes during the prayers, the eulogy, and scripture readings. She wished she could have had a chance to work with her uncle. They would have had a wonderful life together.

When the service was over, she looked at the overflow crowd and realized how highly respected Wilbur Elwood must have been. As they drove to the cemetery she was impressed with the number of cars in the procession behind them. Surely he must have been one of

24

the most prominent men in all of Samoa. First her father and now her uncle; both men should have had years ahead of them. Grief for them both tore through her.

After the graveside service several people surrounded Thayer to express their sympathy. The governor, the minister, and other planters spoke so highly of Wilbur's kindness and generosity that tears filled her eyes again.

She saw Russell approach with the aristocratic stranger who had affected her so peculiarly. He was older and so urbane that she left gauche, schoolgirlish, and almost embarrassed. She hoped the expression on her face in the church had not given her away. A Samoan stopped Russell to speak to him, but the other man stepped toward her, his hands outstretched. Someone mumbled an introduction; she put her hand in his, acutely aware of the pressure of his fingers, his skin against hers.

His eyes, a mixture of brown, green, and gold, unfathomable under the heavy dark lashes, traveled slowly over Thayer, from the silky fall of her hair, to her parted lips, her slightly flushed face, and her slender form.

His prominent cheekbones, strong features, and aggressive chin gave him a commanding, imperious air, as if he were used to giving orders that were to be obeyed without question. Finally he said, "Russell tells me that you need transportation to Nanotuma. I am flying my plane there this afternoon and will be glad to take you. But I'm afraid I'd like to leave as soon as possible. Can you leave in an hour?" He inclined his head and turned away to follow the governor and his party to the limousine waiting in the roadway.

Trembling a little, she watched him go. How impeccably groomed he was in his sand-colored tropical suit, how well built with his broad shoulders and slim hips.

Even after she turned back to the people, her thoughts were on him, and her blood raced happily through her as she realized that she would see him again and would fly with him to Nanotuma. She had never been so fascinated by anyone, so completely enchanted.

After the people had left the graveyard and she was walking back to the car with Russell, he said, "Well, I'm glad you have a chance to go to Nanotuma today. You won't need to wait for the launch."

Another wave of happiness flooded through her at the thought of being with the aristocratic stranger again. "Who is he? We were introduced but I didn't catch his name in the confusion."

"Oh, that's Von. That's what everyone calls him but his name is Eiland von Kuhrt."

Within an hour they were airborne. At first she was tempted to refuse the ride with Eiland von Kuhrt but she had no choice for without funds she had nothing else to do. As she settled herself in the seat next to him she decided that although Von Kuhrt did not resemble the mental picture she had had of him, he was still the man who had nearly ruined Uncle Wilbur and had hastened his death. His virility, suave handsomeness, and outward charm masked a bad character, and she must be on constant guard against his appeal. She was glad that she knew all about him in advance. Yet, in spite of herself, she kept glancing at him, wondering what was going on in his mind.

When Von gained altitude he pointed down to a mountain peak at one edge of the bay on which was built a huge television transmitter tower. "I thought you'd be interested in seeing that tower. The government built it for the educational television system, which is most successful here. Lessons are broadcast in English over six different channels to little schoolhouses

26

all over the islands. That way the classes can be conducted by highly trained instructors here even though the teachers in the remote areas might not be so well educated."

"I've noticed that everyone seems to speak English."

"Yes, especially the younger ones. They all speak Samoan, too, of course." He dipped the wings of the plane. "That high peak is Mount Pioa, the Rain Maker. It's seventeen hundred feet high. People say it must knock all the water out of the clouds because it rains about two hundred inches a year here. You knew that Somerset Maugham's *Rain* was set here in Pago Pago."

"Yes, I know."

As the Cessna leveled and headed northeast, they lapsed into silence, busy with their own thoughts. Thayer looked out the window at the sea below, grateful that she wasn't obliged to carry on a conversation with him, but still she had to admire the capable way he was handling the plane.

Too she had to admit that he had done her a further favor when they were checking out of the hotel and he had told the desk clerk, "Put Miss Elwood's bill on the plantation account." That was fine with her, she told herself grimly, especially in view of the fact that Von Kuhrt was stealing everything in sight and she needed to hoard every cent she had.

In a few minutes Von swooped to a lower elevation and now she could see flying fish leap out of the water, cast a shadow for an instant on the mirrorlike surface, and then dip down to make fountains of sparkling drops.

"You'll soon see Nanotuma," Von said.

She looked below at the empty sea, and then just ahead of them, like an emerald floating on the blue water, was a lushly-vegetated island jagged-edged with

27

coves and inlets. In the center, mountain speaks encircled an extinct volcano crater. Rushing streams and long waterfalls slashed through the dense rain forests that covered the slopes.

A patchwork of taro fields, banana trees, and coconut groves patterned the valleys that extended from the bottom of the peaks to the sea. A barrier reef protected one end of the island, taking the force of the breakers that pounded against it. Inside the reef the calm, clear water in the lagoon mirrored the palm trees along its edge. It was a paradise and she could see why Uncle Wilbur had stayed here so many years.

The plane skimmed over treetops and finally touched down on a runway and came to a stop. Von unbuckled his seat belt, opened the door, and pointed to a pickup parked under a breadfruit tree, which was covered with exotic lobed leaves and heavy fruit. "We'll go up to the house so you can meet my mother. She'll never forgive me if I don't bring you, as she's been anxious to meet you. She loves to have company. Then when you're ready, one of my men will drive you over to your place."

"I'm sorry to be so much trouble." How galling to be under obligation to this man! "Thank you very much."

"It was no trouble. I was flying over anyway."

He helped her out of the plane and carried her luggage to the pickup. "I'll lock up the plane and we'll go."

He returned to the Cessna and brought out a large, cumbersome box, which he placed on the ground while he locked the door. After he put the box in the back of the truck, he explained, "I picked up a part for a pump that's out. We've been waiting for it to come."

As they drove along a road through a thicket of trees festooned with ferns and creeping vines, he continued, "My mother is an invalid. That is why she was unable

28

to come to the funeral with me. She's crippled with rheumatoid arthritis."

And burdened with you as a son, Thayer silently added.

It was hot and sultry in the thicket, but when they emerged and drove along a lush green taro field, Thayer felt the refreshing sea breeze against her damp face. The road dipped down, crossed a wooden bridge over a stream and came up the other side.

They burst through a curtain of ferns and there on a rise overlooking the sea, was the most beautiful house Thayer had ever seen. It was a white two-story French colonial building; across the front were double balconies, one above the other, supported by columns. Between each column was a white railing of intricately patterned iron grillwork.

Acres of green lawn and extensive landscaping surrounded the house. Thayer recognized some of the trees: candlenut, Indian coral with red pea-shaped blossoms, monkeypod, and poinciana looking much like huge scarlet umbrellas. An arm of the lagoon cut inward along one side of the grounds. Around the edge of the inner lagoon were hundreds of hibiscus plants bursting with purple, white, mauve, yellow, and red blossoms, which were reflected by the quiet water.

Instinctively she put her hand on Von's arm. "Stop so I can look at this! I've never seen anything so lovely. I can't believe my eyes! It's magnificent!" Overwhelmed with the beauty, she looked up at him.

He smiled at her appreciatively, and for a moment she forgot her enmity toward him. "I'm glad I brought you this way. You get the best view of the house and grounds from here."

She looked at the house and hibiscus again. "It's so lovely." Embarrassed by her open expression of emotion, she covered her confusion by asking, "When was it built?"

"My grandparents built the house in nineteen ten. Fortunately it was well before World War One so there was no trouble importing the ironwork and other material as well as the craftsmen."

"And the grounds. Those hibiscus."

"The landscaping has been going on all of these years. And you can see why the plantation is named Hibiscus Lagoon."

"It couldn't be named anything else. I'll never forget seeing this place for the first time. The house . . . the sea out there . . . the lagoon, and the hibiscus."

For a moment they were not adversaries but two people who shared an indescribably beautiful sight with complete understanding and appreciation. Then she looked down and realized to her horror that she was still holding his arm. She snatched her hand away. "I'm sorry. You can go on now."

But he didn't start the truck; instead he looked at her with almost a puzzled expression in his eyes, as if she had surprised him with her reaction. "Sometimes I need to see it all from an outsider's point of view to remind me what we have here. I'm afraid I take it all for granted. I've always lived here except when I went to Sydney to university."

"How fortunate you've been, Mr. von Kuhrt."

They drove up to the house and found his mother lying on a chaise on a shady terrace. A wheelchair nearby was the only visible sign of her infirmity. She was tall and slender with streaks of gray in her brown hair and had the same handsome, chiseled features as her son.

"Mother, this is Wilbur's niece, Thayer Elwood. My mother, Mrs. von Kuhrt. I brought Miss Elwood back with me as she wants to stay at Seacrest for a while."

30

"How do you do, my dear. Do sit down." She waved toward a nearby wicker chair that matched her chaise. "I'm still so shocked about Wilbur's death. I just can't get over it. We've been neighbors all of these years."

Thayer sank into a chair completely charmed by this warm, friendly woman.

Von said, "If you ladies will excuse me, I'll change my clothes and get to work. Miss Elwood, I'll send someone to take you over to Seacrest."

His mother spoke up, "You'll do no such thing. She's to stay for dinner and overnight with us."

Thayer protested, "Oh, I mustn't." How could she accept his hospitality and stay under the same roof with him? Mrs. von Kuhrt said, "Tomorrow will be plenty of time to go to Seacrest and cope with that. No, you're to stay here so I can get acquainted with you. What a pretty young lady you are!" She looked up at her son and smiled. "Now take Thayer's luggage into the house and tell Tupuasa that we're having a guest. Tell her also to bring us tea later."

Thayer tried to stop her, but Von shrugged elaborately. "You can't win. She's completely spoiled and always gets her way." He smiled at her indulgently.

"I'm not spoiled, but you are! Now run along. You make me nervous standing there." She waved him away, but instead of leaving, he leaned over and kissed her cheek.

The adoring look Mrs. von Kuhrt gave her son tugged at Thayer's heart. How could such a charming woman have a son capable of doing the things that he had done?

31

CHAPTER 4

As soon as Von disappeared into the house, Thayer felt herself relax; every nerve end tingled with relief. Now she realized how tense and on guard she had been with him. But he was so dynamic and powerful, so capable of outwitting her that she realized just how dangerous he could be.

Mrs. von Kuhrt said sympathetically, "What a time you've had, my dear. Coming all that way to be with Wilbur and then to have him die just before you got here."

"It was a strange thing, but on the flight from Hawaii to Pago Pago I had a premonition that something awful had happened. But I never dreamed that poor Uncle Wilbur—" Her chin quivered and she fought for control.

Mrs. von Kuhrt put her hand over Thayer's. "And you were all alone in a strange country. I don't see how you ever managed."

"Well, Russell McLeod met me at the airport and helped me. You must know him." When Mrs. von Kuhrt nodded, Thayer told her about his kindness.

"He's a fine young man! Now if I were thirty years younger, I'd set my cap for him! He's just a dear and who could resist that beautiful red hair!"

"I'll always remember how nice he was. And if anyone ever needed a friend, I did."

An older Samoan woman came out of the house carrying a silver tray with a teapot, cups and saucers, and plates of tiny sandwiches and cookies.

32

After Mrs. von Kuhrt introduced them, she instructed her housekeeper to call Seacrest and tell them that Miss Elwood would arrive in the morning.

When they were alone again, Mrs. von Kuhrt said, "Wilbur's housekeeper and mine are cousins. Fetu has been at Seacrest for twenty years and is a jewel just like my Tupuasa."

"Do you think she'll stay on now that Uncle Wilbur is gone?"

"Of course. Von wouldn't consider anything else. You can't neglect a house in this climate or everything would be ruined with mildew." Then she held up her swollen hands. "This miserable arthritis. Thayer, will you pour for us?"

While they had their tea, Thayer thought what a comfort it was to have an older woman to talk to and how much she actually missed her mother. Finally she said, "This is the most beautiful house I've ever seen. Its French colonial, isn't it? It reminds me of ones in New Orleans."

"Yes, it is. Von's grandmother was from a French colonial family in Tahiti. I'm sure she had great influence with the architect. I'll never forget when I saw it for the first time. I just couldn't believe my eyes."

"That's just what I said when I saw it too," Thayer agreed as she refilled their teacups.

"I remember it so well," the older woman began. "I'm from Auckland, New Zealand, and when I was twenty-one, I was visiting friends in Western Samoa. You know that Western Samoa was administered by New Zealand under a League of Nations mandate from nineteen twenty on until it became an independent member of the British Commonwealth in nineteen sixty-two."

Mrs. von Kuhrt settled herself more comfortably and went on, "Anyway I happened to be in Apia, the capital of Western Samoa, with my best friend, Barbara Scribner. Her family received an invitation from the Von Kuhrts to come to a ball here at Hibiscus Lagoon. As a houseguest I was included, of course. How thrilled we were! Especially me. I'd never been to American Samoa before but even I had heard about the legendary Von Kuhrts and their plantation here on Nanotuma. We all knew that their son, Gunther, was the catch of the season. Only twenty-five and supposed to be quite handsome."

"You'd never met the Von Kuhrt's before?"

"No. We came in the Scribner's yacht and entered an opening in the reef into the outer lagoon. We anchored out there as many other guests did who came in boats." She laughed gaily. "When I looked up and saw this house, I made up my mind right then that I was going to marry Gunther and live here."

Thayer thought how gay and beautiful Mrs. von Kuhrt must have been at twenty-one. No wonder she'd captured the prize bachelor of the season.

"And what about the Scribners? Did they forgive you for snatching the son and heir from their daughter?"

"Oh, yes. Actually Barbara was very much in love with a young doctor in Auckland. She married him later and we're still close friends."

Caught up in the story, Thayer laughed with the older woman and asked, "Was Gunther as handsome as you expected?"

"No. He was rather stodgy-looking as a matter of fact. Fortunately Von is much more handsome. But Gunther was very nice."

"Did he ever know that you were determined to marry him so that you could live here?"

"Heaven forbid! Indeed not. Poor Gunther took himself very seriously. He always thought that he pursued me." The laughter faded Mrs. von Kuhrt's eyes as she put her cup and saucer down on the table and stretched out on the chaise. "Well, I've been punished for my conniving. Actually this climate does not agree with me. It is too damp and aggravates my condition. I should live where it's very dry like it is in the outback of Australia. But I have no regrets. My husband and I were very happy until his death five years ago."

"And you've had all this beauty to enjoy."

"Yes, and I've had Von. Fortunately he was working for my husband at the time of his death so he was able to take right over."

Thayer hoped that Mrs. von Kuhrt would never know how Von had cheated Wilbur. How many others had been forced to ruin by this man?

Unaware of Thayer's thoughts, the older woman went on. "Gunther was a good man but he had very little joie de vivre. Fortunately Von inherited some of mine. And much of his father's fine character and ability," she added loyally.

They talked until Mrs. von Kuhrt said, "I always go to my room about this time to rest and change before dinner. You must be weary too after your long, difficult day. I'll have Tupuasa show you to your room. Come here to the terrace about seven thirty for a drink before dinner."

"I hope I haven't tired you."

"Indeed not. I've adored it. I want you to come to see me often. I have always longed for a daughter, but it wasn't to be." A maid appeared and helped her into a wheelchair, and they headed for the terrace door.

The interior of the house was as beautiful as the outside. Delicate Chinese rugs covered the polished parquet floors. The furniture was a blending of fine Oriental and European antiques.

As Thayer followed the housekeeper up the stairs to one of the guest rooms, she wondered if some unsuspecting girl would fall in love with the house, as Mrs. von Kuhrt had done, and marry the heir just to live here. She felt sorry for anyone who'd be stuck with the present Eiland von Kuhrt. Of course no one would be wise to him at first; even she had found him attractive until she knew who he was. Naturally her uncle would be taken in by his charm too. He'd been such a close friend of Gunther von Kuhrt, so of course he would trust the son.

Hadn't Wilbur prospered while the older Von Kuhrt was alive? She recalled the attorney's words: "For the past five years he went downhill and just plunged deeper and deeper into debt." Was it just a coincidence that it began with Gunther's death and when the present Eiland von Kuhrt took over? Thayer doubted it very much. She was more determined than ever to find out how Von brought about Wilbur's downfall.

She was too tense to sleep but she took the quilted silk spread off the bed and slipped between the cool percale sheets. She realized then that the house was air-conditioned but not chillingly so. As she rested she thought of how galling it was to accept Von's hospitality on top of the airplane ride here to Nanotuma. She didn't want to be further obliged to him yet another part of her was grateful to be with someone like Mrs. von Kuhrt, for she was desperately lonely and frightened. It was all very well to make brave resolves but carrying them out was another matter, and Eiland von Kuhrt was a formidable adversary with all the advantages of his wealth and connections.

When she joined the Von Kuhrts on the terrace, Von rose from his seat and said, "*Talofa!* That's a Samoan greeting that you'll hear many times." He raised his glass. "May I fix you a drink? What would you like, Miss Elwood?"

His mother spoke up, "Von, for heaven's sake call

36

her Thayer. She's going to be our neighbor and come to see me often, so you don't have to be so formal." Then she winced with pain as she changed her position on the chaise. "You look lovely, dear. What a becoming dress."

"Thank you." Thayer sat down at a chair near the older woman and crossed her ankles. She was conscious of Von looking at her bare feet in their pale green sandals, then his glance traveled up her long slender legs. Her matching green dress clung to her slender body and was almost too revealing against her waist and her softly curved breasts. He looked at her mouth, moist and desirable, and her thick dark hair that curled under ever so slightly and framed her porcelain skin. A slight, self-conscious flush darkened her face.

Von turned then and busied himself at the portable bar. She could see his strong muscles rippling under his blue shirt that matched his trousers. In spite of herself she felt an increasing quickening of her heartbeats. She had never met a man who affected her so physically, and as she clenched and unclenched her fists, she hated herself for her weakness.

As Mrs. von Kuhrt sipped her drink, she said, "I was telling Von that you majored in floriculture in college." In her white caftan edged in gold with matching slippers she was every inch the beautiful, charming chatelaine of the manor house.

Thayer looked at her with admiration. How often she must force herself to move and keep going in spite of the pain. It would be so easy to give in and become bedridden.

Von handed Thayer the drink. "What courses did you have?"

"Well, naturally there was botany. And plant pathology, genetics, propagation, taxonomy, hybridization, morphology, greenhouse management and a lot of

37

things like that. Of course I had to have the usual liberal arts classes too. With a floriculture major, I concentrated more on the science of ornamental plants while you probably went in more for vegetable and fruit crops."

He explained that his major in university was agribusiness. He needed courses such as land management, accounting, and agricultural engineering and exporting rather than general agriculture. "We're limited in the kinds of crops we can grow here in the tropics. I needed broader training. There are always experts like Russell to help with specific agricultural problems."

Mrs. von Kuhrt spoke up, "Von has hundreds of employees. Just keeping an eye on them is a big job."

"I get a lot of help from the *matais*." He sat down near his mother and twirled his glass with his long strong fingers.

"Don Alo was telling me about the *matai* system," Thayer said. "I didn't realize that you had to lease your land and couldn't own it."

He nodded. "I lease most of my land. However, this plantation, Hibiscus Lagoon, belongs to Mother and me. When Baron von Kuhrt came in eighteen fifty, Germany controlled Nanotuma and he was able to purchase this land, but that is no longer possible. I believe that only three percent of the land in Samoa is privately or government owned. The rest belongs to the various Samoan *aigas* or family clans under the tenure of the *matais*. The Samoans very wisely kept control of their land, otherwise it would all be owned by outside interests by now."

His mother added, "We can't sell this plantation. When there are no more Von Kuhrts, the title reverts to the Upos, who are the largest family group on Nanotuma."

Von went on, "They own most of this end of the island. What Wilbur and I don't lease from them, they cultivate themselves. They're excellent farmers."

"Do you have trouble getting laborers?"

"No, the *matais* see to that. They get a percentage on the gross return from the crops so it behooves them to see that we planters have plenty of help."

Thayer settled back in her wicker chair. "Somehow this all reminds me of the plantations in the Deep South in the United States before the Civil War." She could imagine the Von Kuhrt men owning hundreds of slaves and mistreating them.

"I can assure you that there is no resemblance whatsoever," Von said with an edge of annoyance in his voice as he got up to freshen their drinks. "In the first place all income collected by the *matai* is shared by the whole family group. The *matai* is elected or chosen by the family to represent it. Of course he is the chief and the most important person in the family, but if the others are dissatisfied with him, they kick him out and get someone else. The title is not inherited like an Indian chief's."

"I see." Thayer felt a little chastened.

"And don't forget the watchful eye of the Samoan government and the Department of Interior. Every worker must be accounted for, paid the prevailing wage, and given a half-dozen fringe benefits. The planter still pays whether there is a crop failure, hurricane, flooded market, or whatever. It's not an easy way to earn a living, I can assure you."

She had to admit that it would be very demanding to run several plantations and keep them all solvent. It would take management skills, brains, and years of experience.

Mrs. von Kuhrt interrupted. "Von, after dinner you must take Thayer out to the orchid greenhouses. She would be very interested, I'm sure."

39

Von looked at her and asked, "Would you like to see them, Thayer?"

"Yes, please."

As she watched him gather up their glasses and put them on the bar, she wished he weren't so attractive, so intelligent, so full of magnetism and charm. But she reminded herself that appearance and personality could be very deceiving. Some of the most dangerous criminals were also fine-looking and charming. They used their appeal as part of their stock-in-trade. Uncle Wilbur was in the position to judge, and she mustn't fall prey to Von's surface appeal but be ever on guard against his real character underneath.

When dinner was over and Mrs. von Kuhrt settled before the television in the library, Thayer and Von walked along a path toward a group of buildings hidden from the house by shrubbery and trees.

Von's flashlight was hardly needed because the full tropical moon cast a shimmer over the path and the rolling sea, highlighting the crest of each wave until it lapped against the shore. Silver light bathed the quiet lagoons and the grounds surrounding the manor house. A gentle breeze stirred the palm fronds until they rubbed and rustled against each other. From the darkened top of a candlenut tree a night bird called out plaintively. It was an enchanted night.

For a moment a cloud drifted over the moon and they were in darkness. Von took her elbow and murmured, "Don't stumble. Sometimes there are pebbles on the path that turn your ankle."

"I'm all right." But she wasn't at all; she was too aware of his hand on her elbow, his arm brushing against hers and the crazy way her heart was pounding. For an instant she forgot her antagonism and wished he would hold her close. Frantically she asked herself, *What is the matter with me? Am I suffering from moonmadness? This is Eiland von Kuhrt who was the cause of Uncle Wilbur's fatal attack.* Then all her resolve came rushing back.

Fortunately they were soon at the entrance to a long greenhouse. When Von snapped on the light, Thayer gasped with delight. Hundreds of orchids in bloom formed a mosaic of color. Pendulant Dendrobiums hung from tree branches; strap-leaf Vandas grew in large containers filled with volcanic cinders; cane orchids were mounted in hapuu logs; and fire orchids flamed in one corner.

Everywhere she looked was beauty. Miltonias, Lady Hamiltons, and Cattleyas vied with each other for her attention. She touched the velvety petals of the blooms as if to convince herself that they were real. She could smell the damp, pungent moss and hear water dripping from a faucet.

As a floriculturist she looked around at the well-equipped building with admiration. Finally she asked, "Do you really need a greenhouse in this climate?"

"Only to protect these orchids from the winds. And of course some varieties require partial shade." He tested one plant for moisture. "We have a plastic cover that can be rolled down over this greenhouse roof when it rains, so this also serves as a workroom."

"Do you grow these orchids commercially?"

"Yes, but we sell the plants rather than the blooms. Oh, sometimes when I'm flying over to Pago Pago, I have the girls pack a box of blooms and I put them on a plane to Sydney or Auckland. But it wouldn't pay to try to fly them out of here on a regular basis."

"But I suppose the plants can be packed in moss and shipped by boat."

"Yes." He followed her around the greenhouse and pointed out special varieties. Finally he headed toward

41

a door. "We have another greenhouse and a potting shed. Do you want to see them?"

How well-planned the buildings were; regardless of his dealings with her uncle she had to admire Von for the management of his own estate. If only she and Uncle Wilbur could have worked out an operation like this.

Before she thought, she said, "This makes me sad to see all this. Uncle Wilbur and I were going to raise orchids."

He whirled around and stared at her in astonishment. "What do you mean?"

"We were going to grow orchids commercially too. Actually that's why I came." She looked at a shelf of white and red Oncidiums; no wonder they were called "dancing ladies," for she could see how their petals formed puffed sleeves and full shirts.

She glanced back at Von, wondering at his bewilderment. Finally he asked, "Wilbur was really going to establish something like this?"

She nodded. "That's right. I didn't come for a visit. I came to work." Puzzled at his attitude, she wondered if he was incredulous or angry. What difference did it make to him if she and Uncle Wilbur were going to grow orchids too? Surely they wouldn't have interfered with his project.

Von put his hand against a shelf and leaned on it, his face a thundercloud. "If that's true, then Wilbur Elwood was even a bigger fool than I thought!"

As she gasped with shock, anger flamed through her. Her face reddened and her eyes snapped as she cried, "How dare you talk about my uncle that way."

"Because it's true."

"That's unforgivable of you."

"It's a fact nonetheless."

Seething with fury, she stepped toward him. "We just

42

buried him today, yet you badmouth him like that! You're hateful!" She raised her hand and gave him a resounding slap on the cheek.

He grabbed her arm and held it in a viselike grip. There was a dangerous glint in his dark eyes. "I'm warning you—never do that again!"

If I were a man he'd knock me down, she told herself as a flicker of fear ran through her. She said aloud, "You have no right to talk like that!"

She struggled to free herself, but he held tighter. "Let me go!" They glared at each other, and hostility sparked like an electric current between them. She had a hunch that he was going to start shaking her. His body tensed and there were two spots of color in his cheeks; his knuckles whitened as his fingers pressed into her flesh. From the cold fury of his expression she realized what a dangerous enemy he could be.

She yanked at her arm again, trying to free herself, and he snarled, "You little hellcat!"

Anger drove out any discretion and she snapped, "What's the matter with you? Are you afraid Uncle Wilbur and I would have given you a little competition?"

He gave her a shake, then bit words off through tight lips. "Of course not! But for the past five years Wilbur let his plantation go to hell. Got way above his head in debt. Then why would he take on a risky undertaking like raising orchids? Did he want to lose more money?"

"Of course he didn't want to lose money. And why shouldn't it be successful? I would help him." She stared at him defiantly. "I suppose you would see to it that we failed!"

"That remark was uncalled for, Miss Elwood." His face was close to hers.

"Your remarks are uncalled for too!"

His eyes glinted as he gave her another shake. "I es-

43

tablished this to please my former manager who'd retired and wanted to try it. I can afford to take a chance so I did. We've been at this for two years and are just beginning to break even."

"But Uncle Wilbur and I together—"

"There must be fifty thousand dollars invested around here." He nodded toward the orchids. "Where was Wilbur going to get that kind of money? The bank wouldn't let him have it. Were you furnishing the capital as well as the expertise? If so, I apologize."

"Of course I wasn't going to furnish any money. I don't have any. Now let me go. You're hurting me."

He released her arm and she rubbed it to ease the pain from the grip of his strong fingers. Finally she said, "I want to leave. Will you please have someone drive me over to Seacrest?"

"No!"

There was a finality about the single, explosive word that warned against further argument.

"I think you're despicable!"

"Miss Elwood, I could care less what you think. But you're my mother's guest and she'd be very distressed if you left. And no one upsets my mother at Hibiscus Lagoon. Do you understand?"

She fought back angry tears. This heartless man was quite capable of destroying anyone who crossed him. She disliked him more intensely than ever. But she remembered Don Alo's warning to be very careful. When he snapped, "We're going to my office," she followed wordlessly, afraid to disobey. But someday, she vowed to herself, she'd get the best of him.

He turned off the lights, locked the outer door, and headed toward another building in the cluster. She trailed along, wondering what was in store. Why go to his office? Perhaps he wanted them both to cool down before they faced his mother. It would be difficult to be

44

with her just now. How could such a charming lady have a son like Eiland von Kuhrt? He might look like his mother, but there the resemblance ended.

When they came to a building with a night-light over the door, Von found a key on his ring and unlocked it. He led the way through an outer room into a large office paneled in a light tropical wood. Exquisite woven mats, tapa cloth imprinted with ancient designs, and ceremonial masks hung on walls. A huge window looked out on the sea, still silvered by the moon. This room was Von's all right, she thought to herself. Male-oriented, the true setting for a dictator. Here he could sit and hand out orders to the hundreds of peons that worked for him. She remembered Uncle Wilbur's words in his letter, "He thinks he's the all-powerful King of the Universe"; well, this was a proper throne room for His Highness.

He nodded toward a chair near his massive desk. "Sit down." Just like that—"Sit down"—no "please" or anything else, she thought. What a bully.

For a while he paced around the room, rubbing his hand over his thick brown hair, making it look rumpled and boyish; he looked as if he were trying to come to a decision. Finally he perched on the corner of his desk, his anger apparently gone. "I apologize for speaking unkindly of your uncle. I was out of order, I admit. Especially since we just buried him today."

"I doubt if we will see much of each other, Mr. von Kuhrt, but when we do, you're never to make such remarks in my hearing." Although it trembled slightly, she thrust her chin high in the air. "I won't stand for it!"

As he rubbed his cheek a faint smile softened his face. "I can believe that!" He leaned toward her, took hold of her arm, and looked at the red angry marks made by his fingers. "I apologize for hurting you too."

45

She snatched her arm away. "I'm not apologizing for anything. Now can we go back to the house?"

"Not quite yet. I have a business proposition to discuss with you."

He was probably thinking up some other scheme to cheat her further on her inheritance. No doubt there were a few dregs left and he was determined to get them.

"I regret that we've gotten off to such a bad start," he began.

And whose fault is it? Only yours, Mr. High-handed von Kuhrt, she scowled.

He went on. "Well, to be frank, in spite of everything, I would like to have you come to work for me."

"Work for you?" she gasped and sat up, her back ramrod straight. "No way! Absolutely not!"

He held up his hand, leaned forward, and went on. "Now wait a minute. Just hear me out. I need someone to manage my orchid department. Someone who is really trained. A floriculturist like yourself. The old man who started this whole project had little schooling but he was a genius with plants. But his health failed and six months ago he moved to Tutuila to live with his daughter. I put another man in his place, but he doesn't like it. Besides, I need him someplace else."

How could she possibly work for him? She shook her head. "I've had no experience with orchids."

Von got off the desk, paced around, and then rapped out sharply, "With your background you can learn, can't you? I don't expect you to grasp it all overnight. My employees will help you." He stopped by her chair and glared at her, his eyes like dark steel. "You're so damn confident you could've raised orchids successfully with Wilbur, why can't you work for me?"

"Because I don't want to, Mr. von Kuhrt. I'd rather starve first," she said haughtily.

46

"Get off your high horse!" he snapped, his eyes blazing again. "If you expect to stay on at Seacrest, you may have to accept me as an employer whether you like it or not! I can assure you that there's no one else on Nanotuma that has need for a beginning floriculturist. Nor in all of Samoa, if the truth were known!"

That really shook her. She had to have a job, and she wasn't trained for any other kind of work. She had to earn some money. She couldn't even buy a ticket to leave Samoa.

Von went on. "I can offer you a good salary." He quoted a surprisingly high figure. "And you'll have full authority as long as you get results. I won't interfere. I'm far too busy with more important matters."

She glared at him and said sarcastically, "Oh, I'm sure you are."

He straightened up and glanced at his watch. "It's time we were getting back. Mother won't go to bed until she says good night to you. Well, what about it? Will you accept my offer? You'd better make up your mind because I'm not going to ask you again."

She rose from her chair. "It galls me to think about it, but I'll take the job."

"Then we're even. I wish I could find someone else too. But I've tried for six months without any luck. You're here, available, and trained to do the job. I need your help." He took his keys out of his pocket. "Obviously you need the job. They're very few and far between out here. So let's put up with each other."

With a sinking heart she faced reality. She had to work, even if it meant being employed by this impossible man, her uncle's enemy. "All right, Mr. von Kuhrt. I have no other choice. But I want it understood that I have complete authority over the orchid department. I don't trust you for one minute so I want it in writing with your name signed on it."

47

"All right." He jammed the keys back in his pocket, snatched the cover off the typewriter, and wrote a statement. He signed it and gave it to her.

He shrugged and said, "Mother insists that we call each other by our first names."

"I'll think about it. Now let's get back to the house."

He grabbed her shoulder. "You'd better shape up! I won't put up with any surliness from you. Let's get that straight right now! I'm the boss here at Hibiscus Lagoon, and what I say goes. I expect courtesy and respect from all my employees, including you." There was a hint of violence in his manner, and she felt uncomfortable.

She was so infuriated, her voice shook. "Don't worry, you'll get your money's worth." To herself she vowed that she'd use every possible penny of her salary to hire a lawyer to fight him. She'd win out too, even if she had to stay here and work for him forever to do it.

Their eyes met again and for a long moment their anger sparked between them. Then suddenly he pulled her toward him, put his arms around her, his hand against her back and crushed her to him. She could feel the warmth of his body molded against hers and sense his heartbeat. Her breath came fast and her lips parted to cry out in protest, but the next instant his mouth was on hers.

It was a savage, primitive kiss that bruised her lips until stabs of pain shot through her, but every shred of self-control left her; the very blood in her veins caught fire, and wave after wave of longing for him washed over her with a rush of mindless delight and an urgency that matched his own.

CHAPTER 5

The next morning, to her dismay, she realized that Von was driving her to Seacrest. She'd hoped that one of his workmen would be meeting her at the front entrance, where she waited with her packed luggage, but it was Von himself at the wheel of the pickup when it drove up, looking particularly handsome in light khaki work clothes and wearing a wide-brimmed planter's hat.

"Good morning, Thayer," he said with false heartiness. "Are you ready to go to your *fa'atoaga*? That means 'garden' or 'plantation' in Samoan." Apparently he was anxious to get on a businesslike relationship. As he climbed out of the truck he avoided her eyes but he did notice the dark bruises on her arm.

"Good morning, Von," she answered, being careful to use his given name. "Yes, I'm looking forward to seeing the plantation. I've heard about it all my life." It irked her to be so polite.

While he stowed her luggage in the back, she settled herself on the seat and her mind went back to the night before. As soon as Von had released her from his embrace, she had run out of the office building and along the moonlit path to the house. She stopped for a moment in the library to say good night to her hostess and thank her and then rushed to her room.

With the door shut safely behind her she had stood in the dark, looking at the moon, while bitter tears ran down her cheeks as she was overcome with shame. There was something primeval about Von's savage maleness, about his passionate kiss, that had aroused and shaken her. If he had led her to the big couch in his office, she doubted if she could have resisted him.

During her sleepness night she'd thought her situation over carefully. From now on she would be businesslike, impersonal, and polite. She'd keep her true feelings to herself and never again give him reason to call her surly or hellcat. Most of all she would never be caught in his arms again and succumb to his masculine appeal. Her cheeks burned when she thought of how she had responded to him.

By fair means or foul she'd hold on to her job to save money for attorney fees and have the time to search her uncle's records to get evidence. The day would come eventually when she'd be ready. "You just wait, Mr. Eiland von Kuhrt," she said aloud. "You'll be in for the surprise of your life!" But in the meantime she'd use self-restraint even if it killed her, for Von wouldn't put up with much from her, she was sure of that.

When they were on their way, she glanced up at him, wondering if he was thinking about last night too. She asked casually, "How far is it to Seacrest from here?"

"About three miles. Double that if you go by boat because you have to swing around Baron's Point."

"Named after your ancestor, I suppose."

"That's right."

She muttered to herself, *That figures*, but aloud she said, "I hope there's a car of Uncle Wilbur's that I can use to drive back and forth."

"There's a VW, a Jeep and a Ford pickup. Wilbur also came over in his motorboat many times. You might learn to use that. There's plenty of gasoline and diesel on the plantations for the farm machinery, so just help yourself."

Once again she looked up at him out of the corner of her eyes and studied his face. She could see his deep-set eyes and heavy brown eyebrows that matched his mustache. His face was tanned to a golden color with a tiny scar showing white near his ear. Had he fallen off of a horse or out of a tree when he was a little boy? She'd never find out because she had no intentions of asking him.

Von went on. "I spoke to Alefosio this morning. He's been managing the orchid department and he's delighted that you're taking over. He'll stay on for a few days and show you the ropes."

"Shall I start tomorrow?"

"If you will, please. Come about eight. It's best to work in the cooler part of the day in this climate."

Von turned the pickup onto a side road to the left. "We're going by the native village—I want to talk to the *matai*. I hope you don't mind waiting a few minutes."

"No, of course not."

The road cut through the bush—a tangle of weeds, hanging vines, ferns, and trees, such as cocoa, mango, and breadfruit. When they came to a clearing, nestled in a curve of a bay, Von parked in the shade of a gray-barked Barringtonia tree.

"I won't be long. You wait right here in the car."

She almost choked with annoyance. The nerve of him to order her to stay in the car as if she were a small child. Why couldn't she explore the village while she was waiting for him? He was the bossiest, most domineering man she'd ever met. Here on Nanotuma he was a complete dictator with no one to challenge his authority. How could she ever work for him? At least she had her signed agreement that she was in charge of the orchid department. She had it safely zipped inside her purse and she'd take it to work too and show it to him if he tried to throw his weight around.

As she watched him stride across a grassy meadow

toward the village, she mimicked, "You wait right here in the car." Her employment didn't begin until the next day. What right did he have to tell her what to do? She could hardly wait to get to Seacrest to get rid of him.

Soon a dignified, white-haired man, apparently the *matai,* came out of the largest building and walked toward Von with his hand outstretched in greeting. The upper part of the chief's muscular body was bare, but a long skirtlike lavalava tied around his waist covered his legs. Then the two men paced slowly back and forth in the meadow deep in conversation. At least Von didn't act patronizing, Thayer conceded, for he was listening carefully as the chief talked and gestured.

But antagonism flared up in her again. Why had Von parked here instead of driving into the center of the village? Did he do that deliberately to discourage her from talking to the Samoans? She was tempted to get out of the car and walk around the hamlet in spite of his orders. She put one leg out of the truck, then another, ready to slide out of the seat.

She'd found out last night that Von had a short fuse, and he'd made it perfectly clear that he would tolerate no insubordination from her. She decided not to push him too far or she'd end up without a job, in spite of her training and his need for her services. With a sigh she settled back in the seat.

It was very hot and muggy, but soon she was engrossed in observing the interesting scene across the meadow. About twenty-five families lived here, she judged. The open-sided houses, which she had read were called *fales,* were built under a cluster of coconut palms that provided shade. Some of the *fales* were round and others oval-shaped, but each one rested on a raised platform made from volcanic scoria stones. Stout poles supported the top-heavy thatched roofs.

Apparently there was no attempt to insure privacy, for Thayer could look right into the one-room houses. She could see a mother nursing her baby at her breast. In another *fale* an older woman sat on the floor, weaving a basket; a slim, graceful girl in her teens swept while a man squatted on his heels, working with a tool.

How different it was from cooler climates where privacy was so highly prized. Her own home had been built so the rooms looked out on a secluded garden. She remembered how her mother always pulled the drapes before she turned on the lights. Here the unconcerned Samoans went about their business of living in plain view of anyone who wanted to watch them.

Enthralled, Thayer noticed a young mother put dishes in a round tub and then motion to two naked little boys. They walked out of their house toward a communal water tap located about a hundred yards away. The mother put down the tub, turned on the faucet, and sprayed each little boy with a hand-held shower head. She rubbed them all over with soap, rinsed them off, then with a loving swat on their bottoms sent them running around in the hot air to dry. Another woman joined her, and they chatted as they washed their dishes with the sprayer. Finally she called her boys to her and headed back to her open-air house. It was all so natural and without pretense.

In the center of the village was a wooden church with a bell tower where she could attend Sunday services. That would be a good way to get to know the Samoans for she knew that they were devout Christians and their church was the center of their lives.

In an open area there was a school with playground equipment on which some children were climbing. Along a street were three stores and some outdoor stalls where women were shopping. Too she noticed long

53

piers built over the bay with latrines at the end, and she remembered she'd read that these sanitary facilities were placed over water to prevent hookworm.

She watched the people moving around in the village and determined to come back here soon and look all she pleased. His Highness, Mr. von Kuhrt, couldn't control every minute of her day. She'd be under his thumb only eight hours a day, five days a week, thank goodness. The rest of the time was hers.

Finally Von and the old Samoan headed across the meadow toward the truck so Thayer climbed out of it as they approached. A half-dozen brown-skinned youngsters trailed along behind the man, and although they giggled and stared at her curiously, they stayed back at a respectful distance.

When the men reached her, Von said formally, "Miss Elwood, may I present Mr. Malietoa, the chief of the Upo family."

They shook hands and the *matai* said, *"Talofa!* On behalf of my people I welcome you to Nanotuma. But our hearts are heavy with great sorrow because we have lost our beloved friend, Wilbur Elwood. We extend our deep sympathy to you and want you to know that all of us share your loss."

The words were said with such sincerity by the kindly old man that tears flooded her eyes. She struggled for control and finally said, "Thank you. It is particularly sad for me because I came so far to be with him and share his life on this beautiful island." She wiped her eyes with the back of her hand.

As the chief patted her arm he looked at her with sympathy. "We are holding a memorial service for him right after church on Sunday. I hope you will join us."

"Thank you. Certainly I'll be there."

"Your housekeeper, Fetu, will bring you. You will hear of the many things Wilbur did to help us over the years. He was kind and good and we will honor his memory *fa'a Samoa,* in the Samoan way." He turned to Von then and shook hands. "I won't detain you longer. *Soifua!*"

When they were on their way again, Von said, "I could have stopped on the way back from Seacrest to do my business and not kept you waiting. But that would not have been in keeping with the Samoan way. The *matai* would have been deeply offended. He is the chief, the head of the family, and should be the first to welcome you and to be the one to express the sorrow they all feel."

Her neck reddened at his words as he went on. "There is strict protocol here. When they say *fa'a Samoa* or "in the Samoan way," it is more than just custom—it means the courteous or proper way to act. Now if you had gone around and talked to people in the village before the *matai* had greeted you, he would have been insulted. But you'll learn these practices as you go along. I know he was well-impressed with you. You'll be the main topic of conversation in the village now."

"Oh, no!" In spite of herself she laughed. "I think it is so charming that they live so openly. Apparently they don't care if people watch what they're doing."

"I'm sure they'd like privacy as well as anyone else. But they very sensibly build their houses to take advantage of the trade winds. They prefer cool air to privacy—and you can't blame them in this climate."

By now they were back on the main road. Finally Von pointed to the left where a crew of men were working in the fields. "This is the beginning of Seacrest Plantation. We've been grubbing out all of the banana trees and burning them. Then we'll have to disinfect the soil. The bananas were full of scab moth and a virus disease called bunchy top. It's too bad that they got such a hold here. We must get them under control as

55

soon as possible so they won't spread to the other plantations. That would be catastrophic because bananas are the main cash crop here."

She bristled at his implied criticism of her uncle's management but she had to admit that so far, Seacrest was a sorry sight. It was nothing like the flourishing, well-tended Hibiscus Lagoon. In fact the fields looked like an invading army had come in and used them for a battleground. Men were uprooting trees and dragging them into piles, where they were ignited. Trails of smoke floated in the air above the burning stacks.

"How long will it take to get a new crop?"

"About a year. You know that a banana branch dies as soon as it produces a bunch. But suckers sprout up from around the main trunk, and they grow and form buds that produce the new crop. As soon as this ground is ready, we'll bring cuttings from my place and plant them. We should have a profitable yield within a year. It's not like a coconut grove that takes six years to bear fruit."

"Are the coconut palms all right here at Seacrest?"

"Fortunately, yes. In fact they're the only crop we have here until we get the bananas in production; even the taro fields are in a bad way. The Mile-a-minute weed has just about taken over. You have to be on the job all the time here in the tropics or your cleared fields revert to bush. If you get slack, you've had it."

"Of course you're implying that Uncle Wilbur was slack," she snapped. "For all we know he might have been ill for some time."

"You might call it illness."

"What do you mean by that? Don Alo told me that Uncle Wilbur had had an earlier heart attack. He probably never got over it." She disliked him more with each passing minute.

56

Von shrugged and didn't answer. He turned in a long driveway, and she could see the plantation house ahead. It was a long clapboard building, painted a soft gray with white trim, and had a wide veranda across the front. It was not a showplace like Hibiscus Lagoon but still it excited her, for it was surrounded by tall palms and overlooked the bay. It had a charm all of its own as it nestled among the trees.

Most important of all it was the first time she had ever possessed anything of substance and she felt a thrill of ownership. Someday she'd have it cleared from all debts and encumbrances and the whole plantation would truly be hers. But for now at least the house would be a haven, a refuge in her turbulent world.

"Look at the beach!" she cried, noticing it for the first time.

"One of the best in Samoa. It stretches all around the bay to the village on the other side. That's one thing we lack at my place. A beach. But when you have a reef that takes the action of the waves, you don't get a beach."

"Well, you have a beautiful lagoon. Even the Von Kuhrts can't have everything."

Von frowned, and she was glad she'd gotten under his skin again. She'd had all of his company she could stand for a while. As they drove by the back of the house she could see a vegetable garden, a chicken house, and a garage. Von parked near the front by a patch of lawn bordered by gardenias and amaryllis.

As she climbed out of the truck a rush of anticipation washed over her. She looked at the house that was going to be her home. For how long? Weeks? Months? Years?

CHAPTER 6

Before Von could turn off the engine, the back door opened and two Samoans, a plump, middle-aged woman and a genial man came out to greet them.

"Talofa!" Von cried as he jumped off the seat. "Miss Elwood, this is Mr. and Mrs. Atamu who take care of the house and grounds here. Fetu and Tofilau. You will be in good hands with them." He reached for Thayer's luggage and placed it on the ground. Then he got behind the steering wheel again, obviously anxious to be on his way.

Fetu, who seemed to be the one in charge, said, "Welcome to Seacrest, Miss Elwood." Her dark eyes swam with tears. "This is a sad time for all of us."

Thayer's chin trembled. "It is especially hard for you two, for you took care of my uncle for so many years." She shook hands with both of them and then turned to Von to thank him, and their eyes met again. For an endless moment she caught a glimpse of primitive longing, startling in its intensity. He blinked and the expression vanished, but with almost savage fury he whirled the vehicle around and drove away.

While Tofilau picked up the suitcases and headed for the back door, Fetu and Thayer followed more slowly. The housekeeper said sadly, "I still can't believe that Mr. Elwood is gone and will never return. It seems like he's just on a trip. Only this morning I wrote something down I wanted to discuss with him."

"After you show me through the house, Fetu, perhaps the three of us could sit down together and I'll tell you about his funeral. Maybe then we'll all be able to realize what has happened, as I'm still in a state of shock too."

"We'd appreciate that, Miss Elwood." The older woman took Thayer's arm. "Come, let's go in the front entrance. I want you to see the living room first. It's such a pleasant room."

The front door opened into a hall that ended with a staircase to the second floor. Through an arch on the right Thayer could see a dining room that looked out on the veranda. The living room, through another arch to the left, was a large sunny room with exposures on three sides. From the front windows one could see across the veranda and lawn to the bay. The side windows looked out on the palm trees and frangipani bushes with big white blossoms and shiny dark green leaves. The back windows revealed a stretch of lawn ending at a stately banyan tree, whose roots, growing earthward from horizontal branches, screened off the garage and other plantation buildings at the back.

Wooden shutters, which were used to shut out the too strong sunlight, were now folded against the walls. The light parquet floors, a Chinese area rug, and handsome rattan furniture attested to former prosperous days. But the walls, now streaked a dirty cream color, badly needed paint; the cushions on the furniture were faded and shabby; and the panel curtains hung limply, as if they had been laundered too many times.

"How lovely this room could be," Thayer said aloud, visualizing its appearance when she redecorated it. The walls should be a pale, cool green and the shutters, white to match fresh sheer panels she'd put at the windows. She'd make new gay covers for the cushions, using material with various shades of green, yellow, and

59

gold. She'd bring houseplants into the room too, airy ferns and green and gold orchids. Someday it would be a delightful place.

As Thayer touched one of the worn cushions she said, "I'd like to make some new covers. Do we have a sewing machine?"

"Yes, ma'am. It's an old treadle machine but it works very well. I sew too and could help you."

"Wonderful. We'll work together."

The housekeeper led the way into the study. A huge rolltop desk, bursting with papers and account books, took up much of the room. Thayer knew she'd be spending hours of time in this room, going through all her uncle's records. Fortunately no redecorating was needed here except for a new couch cover, which would be easy to buy. The walls were paneled in a light Philippine mahogany, and the shutters had been made to match. It was a lovely room, and she could visualize Uncle Wilbur busy at his desk, going over his accounts.

They left the study and walked through the dining room, which would be repainted too, she determined. The kitchen and service porch seemed in reasonably good condition. As they walked up the stairs to the second floor Fetu said, "I have the guest room all ready for you."

It was apparent the walls of her room had been newly painted a soft blue, which matched the water in the bay she could see from her front window. The woodwork and the furniture were freshly redecorated in white.

As Thayer looked around she cried, "This is delightful! I love it." The room, which was above the kitchen and service porch, had windows on three sides. A white tufted spread and crisp ruffled curtains were new. "Did you fix this up for me, Fetu?"

The housekeeper nodded, her dark eyes glowing with

pleasure at Thayer's appreciation. "My husband helped me with the painting."

"It's so pretty. Thank you so much."

"Your uncle wanted everything just right for you. He hoped you'd stay a long time."

"I am going to stay, as this will be my home from now on."

"I'm so glad. We didn't know what would happen now that poor Mr. Elwood is gone." Fetu pointed to a white tiled room with blue and white towels hanging on glass rods. "You have your own bath of course."

Thayer looked around again. "I'll be very happy here. I couldn't be more comfortable."

The remaining room and adjoining bath were obviously the master-bedroom suite used by her uncle. Now it was shuttered and dark. It was shabby and needed redecorating, but they would have to dispose of his things first.

As they walked back down the stairs Thayer said, "This house seems surprisingly cool. Is it air-conditioned?"

"Oh, yes. Mr. Elwood had it installed about eight years ago. We have our own generator that provides electricity for the house and outbuildings. My husband and I live in a house out in back and we have electricity too. Not all Samoans can say that."

"I suppose not."

"If you'll excuse me, Miss Elwood, I'll find my husband and send him to the veranda. Shall I bring us a cool drink and we sit out there and talk?"

"That will be fine." Thayer went out the front door and sat on a porch swing. The cool trade winds from the bay tempered the hot tropical air. Soon Tofilau joined her and sat on the floor at the edge of the veranda. Fetu brought a tray of frosted glasses with fruit juice and passed it around before seating herself in a wicker rocker. Thayer sensed that it would not seem proper to them to gather in the living room. Apparently Uncle Wilbur had held his conferences with them here.

As Thayer sipped her drink she told them in great detail about Wilbur's funeral. She spoke briefly of her own father's death and mentioned the fact that her mother had remarried and moved from Minnesota after selling the family home. She also told of her new position with Eiland von Kuhrt.

"So you see," she concluded, "this is my home now. Uncle Wilbur left it to me. Even though Mr. von Kuhrt is managing the plantation itself, the house is mine." She wanted them to understand that point thoroughly and that she was not here because of Von's charity. She went on. "It's going to take a long time, maybe years, to settle the estate and get all of his affairs straightened out, so I want you two to stay right here and help me take care of this house. You will receive your wages as usual from the plantation account, I understand, as it is important that all the buildings be kept up."

"I'm so glad you want us," Fetu said. "This has been our home for so long. We've been awfully worried."

"Mr. Elwood left a small legacy to you two, but his affairs are so complicated and tied up with the bank that it may be a long time before it can be honored."

Fetu answered, "The main thing is that we have our home and our jobs here. There's not just ourselves but we help so many others in our *aiga,* our family. That's *fa'a Samoa,* to help each other."

Mrs. von Kuhrt was so right, Thayer thought, Fetu was truly a jewel. How fortunate Wilbur had been to have her look out for him all those years. Tofilau seemed to be a genial man, but Thayer suspected he could be lazy and shiftless and only work when Fetu prodded him.

She said aloud, "We'll get everything in first-class condition. First we'll do over the living room and dining room, then sometime later we'll take on Mr. Elwood's bedroom."

Fetu nodded in approval and said, "The poor man let things go these last few years. Lots of things needed doing, but when I told him about them, he kept putting them off. 'Don't bother me now,' he'd say."

Tofilau added, "He wasn't well. God rest his soul."

"The three of us will gradually get things in order. This is a beautiful place and deserves the best of care," Thayer said.

In the afternoon Thayer unpacked her clothes and settled herself. She laid out her slacks and a cool blouse for work the next day and then went downstairs to make sure there was a car in working order. She chose the VW and instructed Tofilau to drive it to the plantation headquarters to fill it with gasoline. By the time she had everything ready, she felt she was prepared to begin a new life.

When she returned to her bedroom, she wondered how difficult it would be to have Von for a boss. No doubt he was just as concerned about having her for an employee. There was a physical attraction, a special chemistry, between them that shocked her. She had never lost such control over her emotions before; her face never flushed with embarrassment so easily. Here he was a total stranger and her uncle's enemy, and yet she reacted to him with such abandon. Von sensed this magnetism between them too, she was sure as she recalled his anger at himself as he drove away. From now on, she reminded herself again, their relationship would be totally businesslike; there would be no repetition of such actions, for she and Von were adversaries, and her purpose in working for him was to bring him to justice.

She sat down in a big white wicker chair and looked around her attractive room again. There was a white painted desk and a chair, a chest of drawers, and dressing table as well as a roomy closet. A blue cotton rug matched the walls.

For the first time since her father's death, she felt settled. With all the changes in her life this past year she had been so disoriented; she had many friends who thrived on being at loose ends, who rebelled at structure and discipline, but that wasn't her nature. She needed order, a pattern to her life, to know what to expect. Perhaps she was extra sensitive to upheaval these last few months, but she had a niche now and felt squared away. This house was more than just a shelter; it was a refuge that was truly her own.

That evening, when Fetu served her dinner in the dining room, Thayer asked, "What about supplies? How do you manage all this delicious food?" She looked at her fruit salad and her plate of roast pork, baked yams, and creamed taro leaves.

"Of course we grow a great deal here on the plantation and all the people who live here are welcome to use anything they need," Fetu explained. "There are twelve homes at the headquarters, which is about half a mile up the bay nearer to the village. On this acreage we raise pigs, chickens, fruits, and vegetables besides the cash crops."

"I didn't know that."

"Also the men go fishing in the bay and we all share what we have. I have a freezer here, then about once a month, I order staples through the grocery store at the village. The bill is sent to the headquarters and the accountant pays it." She continued, "My husband has a vegetable garden and a few chickens for our use here at the house. There's always plenty to eat."

"And you are a splendid cook. Everything tasted so good." Thayer smiled.

"Thank you, ma'am."

When Fetu returned to the kitchen and her own dinner at the dinette table with Tofilau, Thayer finished her meal, deep in thought. So she wouldn't have to pay for food out of her salary, nor for utilities or gasoline; all those expenses were paid by the plantation accountant.

That meant that she could save a great deal every month toward attorney fees and court costs. It would be very expensive to fight a man with Von's power and resources. She'd bide her time and get all her facts together as well as her money saved before she'd act.

She decided to use her own money to fix up this house. Not for the world would she have Von and the bank complaining about any unusual bills.

That evening, when she was in the study, Russell telephoned her. She told him about her job with Von.

"That's great! I couldn't be more pleased. I've been concerned about you. It's just a fluke that you found a job in your line there on Nanotuma."

"But I'm wondering how I'll get along with my boss though. I imagine Von can be very difficult and demanding."

"He is. I won't deny that. But he's fair. If you do your part, you'll get along all right."

She changed the subject and told him about her plans to refurbish the living and dining rooms. "How should I get the material? Do I send to a mail-order house in the States?"

"You can, of course. No doubt there are catalogs around there. But it would take a long time. Perhaps I can find something here in Pago Pago. They might not have much selection but they import goods from Hong Kong and Japan and could have something you'd want.

I'll get samples and mail them to you so you can see. If you find material you like, I could buy it and bring it when I come."

"Marvelous. But you'll have to wait to buy anything until I get paid. I don't want to charge it to the plantation." She described the material she had in mind, the paint and panel curtains.

"I'll see what I can find, Thayer. With that big a project you'll be tied down there all summer at least, so perhaps we can become friends."

"I'll be here indefinitely, Russell. This is my home and I'm fixing it up as nicely as I can make it."

"Good for you! I'll start looking around and write you tomorrow night. But I'd better hang up before this bill gets too astronomical. Good-bye. Take care."

As she replaced the receiver she thought that at least she had one friend here in Samoa. From the very beginning Russell had been helpful and concerned about her.

What a difference there was between Von and Russell. Von upset her and put her on edge, made her feel so uptight; on the other hand Russ was so soothing and gentlemanly. That was the right term—a gentle man, instead of a hard-nosed, domineering one.

She walked out on the veranda and was surprised to find that it was raining, but the air smelled fresh with the fragrance of newly washed plants and damp earth. She could hear the rain pelt on the roof and rush out of the drainpipes.

What was Von doing? Was he standing outside too, watching the rain? Was he also wondering what the coming months would bring?

CHAPTER 7

It was with some trepidation that Thayer started out the next day with her lunch in a brown bag and a Thermos of fruit juice. She wasn't too sure about driving the VW and wished that she'd practiced more around the grounds. Also she wondered if she could find the way alone. It was all so strange and there was so much to learn at once. Even this early it was hot and muggy. Would she ever get adjusted to the tropical climate, her new job, and this strange island?

But she arrived at Hibiscus Lagoon without trouble and was soon parked in the shade of a candlenut tree near the greenhouse. Alefosio proved to be a big, likable man in his early thirties. When she entered the door, he was spraying the orchids with a fine mist of water.

When he saw her, he cried out, "Good morning! You are Miss Elwood who are rescuing me from this no-good job? I'm Alefosio."

As she shook hands she laughed. "Yes, to everything. I'm indeed Thayer Elwood. But that sounds discouraging to call it a no-good job."

"For you a good job! For me terrible. I'm to show you the ropes and then I can get away from all these damn orchids. I'm to be the manager of Masina Faga or Moon Bay Plantation at the other end of the island. That's the kind of a job for me."

"I'm glad I'm taking over, then. But I want to learn all I can from you first."

67

"I don't know much. Taligi and her daughter, Lua, work here too. They know more than I do. It was their uncle, Sasa, who started all this. They'll come along pretty soon." He turned off the spray. "When Sasa left, Mr. von Kuhrt put me in charge here. 'You help me out now,' he said, 'then I'll make you manager of a plantation as soon as I can.' And he did." His round bronze face beamed with pride.

"Does Mr. von Kuhrt come around here often?" Thayer asked, hoping for a negative answer.

Alefosio shook his head. "Not often." He waved his hand at the orchids. "The whole idea is to have a shipment of plants ready every two weeks and at the docks at Falelumu—that's the port across the island. A freighter comes from New Zealand and picks up bananas, coconuts, and these orchid plants. A broker in Auckland airfreights the plants all over the world."

"And if you don't have the shipment at the docks on time?"

Alefosio drew his finger across his throat. "Off goes your head!" He grinned. "I've never missed. That's why mine is still on." But underneath his joking Thayer sensed an awe and wholehearted respect for his boss who obviously put up with little inefficiency.

Then he showed her where the clay pots, fibrous loam, sphagnum moss, osmunda fiber, and insecticides were stored, along with shipping boxes, excelsior, and other supplies. It was a well-organized operation.

"Actually Taligi and Lua do most of the packing for shipment. It's my job to select the plants that are ready to be shipped. Then I drive the truck to Falelumu and make sure the plants are put on the coolest part of the freighter and the crew told how to spray them en route. I'm taking a shipment tomorrow, and you can go with me."

Taligi, a handsome woman in her forties, and her

shy, pretty daughter, Lua, arrived, both dressed in flowered muumuus. Thayer could understand why Russell was so enthusiastic about Samoa, for the people were so warm, friendly, and attractive.

Thayer said. "I'm going to need a lot of help from you people."

Taligi smiled and answered, "Don't you worry about anything. You'll learn all about these orchids as you go along."

Alefosio added, "After all a lot of them grow wild out in our forests without any help from us. They'll survive while you get the hang of things."

But it wasn't that simple, Thayer soon learned. After Alefosio got the women started with the packing of the plants to be shipped, he turned to her. "I'll show you about the repotting. First thing every morning I look the plants over and mark the ones that need repotting with a piece of chalk. Notice this Cymbidium. The roots are potbound and have forced the plant above the rim." He took the plant off the shelf and carried it into the potting room.

After knocking the plant from the pot and carefully lifting it out, he went on. "See how the roots have grown down into the pieces of crockery in their search for food. You have to remove all the pieces of crock and the old compost. Then you must work fresh compost in among the roots."

"Yes, I see that."

"One thing to remember, when you repot an orchid, it should never be put in a container that is too small. So select the right-sized pot, then hold the plant firmly with its rear to the side of the pot to allow room for it to grow forward. Remember, firm potting is important. You must use a potting stick to pack the compost well down into the crevices."

"Okay." She pulled a stool to the bench and sat

down. It was still early in the day but she was already beginning to feel the debilitating effect of the humid heat. It would take some time to become acclimated, she realized.

Alefosio went on. "When the pot is packed three-fourths full with new compost, you should be able to lift the plant by the leaves without the pot falling off. See?" He held the plant in the air. "Then you put more compost in and trim it off and firm down the outer edge."

"Find another plant that needs repotting and I'll see if I can do as well," Thayer said.

After returning the Cymbidium to its place, he selected another plant for her. As she worked he added, "Usually you repot an orchid right after its flowering season and before it pushes out the new roots. That way the young roots can grow into the new compost."

She nodded, then felt the soil. "I notice that this plant is quite dry. I suppose it's best to repot then."

"That's right. Otherwise you'll break off the roots."

As they worked all morning he showed her how to remove worn-out bulbs from the back of the plants, how to cut away the dead roots, and when to use bone meal.

"Don't water a repotted plant for several days, but just spray it lightly to keep the foliage fresh."

In spite of her aching arms and tired back, it was an exhilarating experience. Despite his dislike of his job, Alefosio certainly was good at his task.

Finally she looked up and saw Von in the doorway, watching her, and was instantly on the defensive. How long had he been there? Why wasn't he off doing his important work instead of wasting time here? She was all too conscious of her dirty hands, the smudge on her cheek, and her disheveled hair.

She was unaware that Von was thinking how beautiful she looked with her dark, violet eyes alive with in-

70

terest, her glowing skin, and her thick, blue-black hair that curled ever so slightly in the damp air.

"Be careful that you don't overdo your first day," he said, his voice surprisingly gentle. "After all you came from a temperate climate and you have to get adjusted first."

"I'm finding that out," she said. "Also how little I know. There's so much to learn here. Now I wonder what I was doing for four years at my university."

Von stepped into the potting room. "Well, you got a solid scientific background, which gives you a base for practical knowledge."

Alefosio swept his arm in a wide gesture at all the plants they had repotted. "She learns quick." He snapped his brown fingers. "Just like that she catches on. Right away she'll be able to take over."

As Thayer brushed her hands together to knock off the compost, she laughed. "Don't let him kid you. He's just anxious to get over to Masina Faga Plantation."

Von leaned against the shelf. "I'm anxious to have him too. But it's only fair to have you feel quite at ease before you take over."

Alefosio clapped his hands to his forehead and groaned. "That could take weeks."

Thayer slid off her stool. "This is Wednesday. Supposing you stay with me through Friday. Then let me try it on my own next week with the understanding that I can call on you for help when I need it. Is that all right?" She looked at the two men.

Relief showed in Alefosio's face. "Good!" He turned to Von. "Okay with you, boss?"

Von nodded while he put his hand on the foreman's shoulder. "We'll try it. But it's with the understanding that Miss Elwood's requests take priority over everything else. And I mean top priority."

"That's right. Leave it to me." Alefosio snapped his

fingers again. "You call for me, and I'll come just like that."

"Fine." Thayer stretched her arms over her head. "It takes awhile to find out what you don't know. Right now it's all kind of a blur."

Von said, "Better take a lunch break now, Thayer." He turned to go into the other section where Lua and Taligi were working.

Thayer washed her hands and walked out to her VW to get her lunchbag. She was seated on the grass in the shade, eating a sandwich, when Von found her there later.

He asked, "Won't you come to the house and have lunch with us? My mother would be so pleased. She's taken quite a liking to you."

Thayer shook her head. "Thanks, but I brought my lunch. Besides, I'm one of your employees now, so we'd better start out in a businesslike way. But tell your mother I'll try to stop by and say hello before I go home."

For a long moment the two adversaries looked at one another. As she gazed up at him, towering over her, she was all too aware of how undignified she must look, sprawled in the grass. She was conscious of his strong, square-jawed, and very masculine face, with lines of experience, even laughter, perhaps, on each side of his mouth. His strength, his dynamic personality, his attractiveness drew her to him once again.

As she watched him walk toward the house she sat back with a sigh of relief, releasing her pent-up emotions. What a mixed-up muddle it all was. Why did he have to be the one who destroyed Uncle Wilbur?

Finally she stretched out on the grass, and while she half-dozed, she wondered if she could ever learn all the complexities of orchid culture. How naive she'd been to think that she and Uncle Wilbur could have started a commercial operation from scratch. It was so involved and would take a big investment to get off the ground, one should have years of experience before attempting such a business. What was behind her uncle's thinking?

Right after her lunch hour Alefosio gave her a lesson in orchid propagation so there would always be plants to sell. "Orchids are not rapid growers," he explained. "And there's no use trying to propagate a plant that is too small or weak."

He moved to a special section of the greenhouse, selected two specimens, and carried them to the potting room. As he knocked one plant out of its pot he went on, "With Cymbidiums or Odontoglossums you can remove one or more of these back bulbs if the plant is large and strong. Of course you have to wait until the bulbs have lost their leaves. After you take them off the parent plant, you can pot these bulbs. You must use a fine compost or just put them in chopped sphagnum moss. Be careful you don't plant them too deep."

As she watched his quick hands she asked, "Aren't there some orchids that you can just divide?"

"Yes, the Cattleyas, for example, when they have two leads." He filled a pot with special mixture. "We'll divide some of those and I'll show you what I mean. And another thing, when you notice a Vanda or other stem-rooting orchids producing growth from its side, you can cut that away and plant it. It will become a new plant."

"I'll see if I can find one with side growth."

For a while they worked with the Cattleyas and Vandas, and then he chose another variety. "This Dendrobium is easy to propagate. Look, you just remove this good healthy back growth that is leafless. Then you cut it into lengths of about two inches and stick them around the edge of a four or five-inch pot. When they root, you can repot them."

By the middle of the afternoon Thayer was weary. When she looked up to see a maid pushing Mrs. von Kuhrt in her wheelchair into the greenhouse, she called out, "Am I glad to see you! I need an excuse for a break." She ran to greet the older woman.

Mrs. von Kuhrt sent the maid back to the house and said, "I came to see how you were getting along, Thayer. And I wanted to make sure that Alefosio isn't overworking you."

"I'm not. I swear it. I'm not." The Samoan grinned. "But Miss Elwood learns so fast. She knows more than I do already."

Thayer shook her head. "Don't believe a word he says. He wants to dump this whole operation in my lap so he can cut out of here."

"I'm sure of that. Well, after I see the orchids, I'm taking you up to the house to have tea with me." Mrs. von Kuhrt shook her finger at Thayer. "After all, I own this plantation too, so I can give a few orders."

A rush of gratitude and liking for this kind woman came over Thayer as she answered, "I'd like that. Frankly I'm exhausted. The first day at anything is always so trying. There's so much to learn all at once."

"You must watch yourself until you get used to our climate, Thayer." Then Mrs. von Kuhrt pushed her wheelchair near a tall-stemmed plant bearing at least twenty sparkling white orchids with oval, pointed sepals and petals about the same size. The little bifurcated lips of the blossoms were faintly dotted with purple. "Isn't this one superb?"

"Yes, it is." Thayer leaned over and read the label. "It's a *Caularthron bicornutum* or Virgin Orchid. I guess it's called that because it's so white and pure."

The two women were alone now, and Mrs. von Kuhrt said in a low voice, "Orchids fascinate me. You know, when Sasa first suggested that we build these greenhouses and grow orchids commercially, I was the one that insisted that we do it and even put up part of my private fortune to finance it. I'd hoped to spend a great deal of time here, but it wasn't to be." There was a sad, wistful expression on her face.

"Why not?" Thayer asked

"I wanted Sasa to teach me about them, to let me help him, but I soon found out that I made him awfully nervous and unhappy when I was here. Naturally I quit coming, as he seemed to think I was spying on him instead of trying to learn."

"Oh, that's too bad."

"Then we all knew that Alefosio took over this orchid department to help Von out. I didn't want to add to his dissatisfaction so I stayed away."

"Well, I would love having you around, Mrs. von Kuhrt," Thayer exclaimed. "I mean it! We can learn about orchid culture together. Naturally I studied something about them in my floriculture courses and I can teach you what I know. And I see quite a lot of reference books on orchids in the potting room that we both can read. There's no reason why you can't become an expert!"

"How I would love that! I get bored and feel so useless with so little to do."

Thayer pushed the wheelchair to a bench at the end of the greenhouse and said, "Look at these collectors' items, Mrs. von Kuhrt. When these are ready to be propagated, they'll be very profitable. See this Lockhartia with braided leaves."

"I didn't even know that we had these special plants." The older woman put out her hand and touched the dainty yellow flowers that grew from the axils of the top leaves.

"There's one example of the kind of thing you could do. You could read up on all the new and rare orchids that are being developed and decide on the ones that we could grow on a commercial scale here."

Mrs. von Kuhrt's eyes glowed with interest. "That's true."

Thayer went on. "Beginning on Monday, I'm going to have complete charge of all this. So from then on you plan to spend all the time you can here."

"You can't imagine what that means to me, dear."

Thayer patted her arm and then sat down on a vacant spot on the bench. "Apparently Sasa and Alefosio never bothered with hybridizing, did they? That's what interests me. Developing new varieties."

Mrs. von Kuhrt shook her head. "As far as I know, they never did any crossbreeding. Of course it was all Sasa could do to get this operation going. That was a big undertaking for him. And toward the end he was ill."

"Well, he did an excellent job. I hope I can carry on with his work."

"Of course you will, dear. But once you get the swing of everything, why don't you try hybridizing? I'm sure Von would approve."

"He has nothing to say about it. He signed an agreement giving me complete authority here."

Mrs. von Kuhrt stared at Thayer in astonishment. "What? I can't imagine Von doing that."

Thayer smiled. "Now that I think about it, I can't either. But we had a battle royal out here night before last because he criticized my Uncle Wilbur. Then when Von said I would have complete authority here if I would take this job, I was mad enough to insist on a statement to that effect in writing."

"Thayer, what a delight you are." Mrs. von Kuhrt threw back her head and laughed until tears came to her eyes. Finally she said, "Of course I adore Von but I have to admit that he is a complete autocrat around here. There is no one to challenge his authority, and he's become almost a despot. Just like his father. What he says goes, no question about it. It's unheard of that you got him to write that statement."

"As soon as I take complete charge, I will bring it and keep it here so I can produce it if necessary."

"It will be necessary, I can promise you that." She started laughing again. "I hope you stay forever, dear."

"But of course I won't," Thayer answered. "Von will fire me one of these days, I imagine." She couldn't imagine anything worse than working for Eiland von Kuhrt forever.

CHAPTER 8

The next morning Thayer met Alefosio at the entrance to the greenhouse and said, "I want to go through every step of this shipping procedure so let me go with you to get the truck. I want to start at the beginning so I won't have trouble when I'm doing it on my own."

"Okay, but there's nothing to it. First we go to the plantation office to sign up for the truck and get the keys. We might as well go now."

After they walked to the office and she met the girls who worked there, she signed a request slip for a panel truck. They went on to a shed that held the various plantation vehicles. It was a large building with posts holding up a corrugated roof without walls so the breeze could blow through.

When Alefosio found the proper truck, Thayer said, "Let me take over. I want to fill it with gas, load it, drive, and everything while you're here to show me how. Getting the plants shipped seems to me the hardest part of the whole job."

Alefosio shook his head. "It's not at all. Just relax."

"But you're used to it and I'm not."

"Relax. Take it easy. Don't worry about anything." Alefosio elaborately shrugged his broad shoulders. "Taligi will show you how when I'm gone."

But Thayer knew she wouldn't relax as long as she had to prove herself. She didn't want to make any mistakes to incite Von's wrath, knowing how easy it would be to bring on his disapproval.

When they returned to the greenhouse, they loaded

the orchid plants, which were carefully packed in cardboard boxes that had holes in the sides and tops to allow air circulation. While they worked, Alefosio suggested, "Maybe Mr. von Kuhrt will let you take one of the men to help you on shipping days."

"No!" she snapped. "I'm not going to ask special favors of him. It's been part of your job and it'll be part of mine."

When they were on their way to Falelumu, she tried to memorize the route as she drove across the island. They skirted along the edge of the various plantations and then entered the rain forest as the road wound up a mountainside. When they reached the summit, she could see a small village below with docks built out into a sheltered bay. The road twisted and turned down the face of the cliff.

As she slowly negotiated the hairpin curves she gripped the steering wheel tightly. She tried to laugh as she said, "This is some road."

"You'll soon get used to it. We call it *O le gata,* which means 'the snake.' "

"It's snaky all right. Wow!" When they reached the level road along the edge of the bay, she let out a long sigh of relief. "Well, I made it."

The village of Falelumu was less attractive than other hamlets she had seen, for the *fales* had galvanized metal roofs, many installed right on top of the more picturesque thatching. To weigh the metal down in case of high winds the Samoans had used old tires in pairs joined by a rope, with one tire resting on the front side of the roof and the other on the back. It might be practical but it was ugly, Thayer decided.

A freighter alongside the dock showed streaks of rust on its black hull. Big white letters on the bow proclaimed that it was the *Maori Queen* from Auckland. A long line of Samoan stevedores carried cases of bananas from trucks to a crane that swung back and forth to load the hold.

When they stopped their truck on the dock, Alefosio said, "You'll always find someone hanging around the dock who wants to earn some extra money. They'll unload the truck for you. You pay them and turn the bill in to the office at the plantation." Sure enough, a lava-lava clad young man, his skin shining with perspiration, came up to them, pushing a hand truck, and a deal was soon negotiated.

When they were on board the freighter, ready to turn over their bill of lading to the purser, Thayer could see the crew members looking her over and exchanging glances with each other. One let out a long whistle when he saw her. Even the purser seemed to leer at her.

This was a problem she hadn't anticipated. She hoped she could cope with these crew members when she was on her own and that she would be able to get the plants stored in a proper place and make sure that someone sprayed them on their journey to Auckland. Would they arrive in a salable condition? Would they take her instructions seriously even though she was young and a woman? She hoped they would not sense her insecurities on her first job and take advantage of her. Well, it would be two weeks before she'd have to ship plants on her own, so she could shelve that worry for now.

There were plenty of immediate concerns to keep her busy for the next two days. She tried to foresee every problem and get Alefosio's advice while she still had him with her. She wanted everything to run smoothly right from the start when she took over.

On the way home Friday afternoon she felt almost ill with exhaustion, the humid tropical heat, and tense nerves. Fetu met her at the front door and said, "I have a pitcher of cold fruit juice ready, Miss Elwood.

Wouldn't you like to have some? If you go in the living room, I'll bring it to you."

Thayer wiped her damp forehead. "Thank you. I'd love a drink before I go upstairs to shower."

There was concern in Fetu's dark eyes. "You look very *vaivai*, that means tired in Samoan."

"I'm *vaivai*, all right. I guess it's always hard to start a new job. And of course I'm not adjusted to this climate yet."

Wearily Thayer stretched out on the divan in the living room and looked out at the bay. Tomorrow she'd swim, she decided. But right now she was grateful for the cool, air-conditioned air that surrounded her. The shutters on the south and west windows were closed to the glaring afternoon sun. What a haven this house was. At least she'd always have this place to come home to from her responsibilities at Hibiscus Lagoon and her efforts at pleasing the taskmaster there.

When Fetu brought the fruit juice, she handed Thayer a thick letter. It was from Russell and contained swatches of upholstery material and folders with paint samples that showed he'd done a thorough job of shopping in Pago Pago. She thought of him with a rush of gratitude. What a darling he was.

As she sipped her drink she looked over the upholstery material and found them all attractive. But one in particular appealed to her since it contained the colors she wanted—two shades of green, along with yellow, gold, and just a tiny accent of orange against a white background. The predominant motif of bamboo leaves would give a light, airy feel to the room. But she was shocked at the price; it would be expensive, there was no doubt about that.

However, Russell wrote that the store manager said Wilbur Elwood had always had a personal charge account with them and they would take the liberty of changing it to Thayer's name since she was the new owner of Seacrest. The manager would write her at once, inviting her to order whatever she wanted from them, and they would put it on her charge account. Well, that would make it possible to go ahead with her project right away, she thought. She'd have some paychecks by the time she received the bill.

Russell also said that he'd be coming to Nanotuma at the end of the week in connection with his job and that if she could let the store know what she wanted right away, he could bring the order with him. He always stayed at Hibiscus Lagoon but would like to see her; well, she wanted to see him too. Of course he would never agree with her opinion of Eiland von Kuhrt, but other than that, he was great.

The next day Fetu helped her measure the cushions and seat covers to get an estimate of the material they would need. When Tofilau came in for his lunch, they decided on the color of paint and the number of gallons to be ordered.

Later, as Thayer sat cross-legged on the floor with a yardstick in her hand, she said, "I might as well send for the panel curtains too. Mr. McLeod said there was very little choice."

"I'll be glad to get rid of these at the windows now. They should have been replaced a long time ago. But poor Mr. Elwood——" Fetu's voice trailed away.

Thayer tapped the pencil against her lips. "I want to be sure my order goes out on the launch Monday. Should I drive over to Falelumu with it today or tomorrow?"

Fetu shook her head. "That isn't necessary. We'll take it to the post office box in the village and mail it when we go to church tomorrow. The storekeeper, who also is the postmaster, meets the launch every Monday and Friday, and he'll send it with the other mail."

Thayer spent the afternoon on the beach in front of her house. She swam in clear, refreshing water, feeling that she was truly in paradise. If only Uncle Wilbur had lived so they could have enjoyed it together. She was rapidly growing to love Samoa and even getting more adjusted to the tropical climate.

The next morning Thayer dressed carefully for the memorial service in her pale yellow jersey with a matching scarf over her dark hair. Fetu wore a *pule-tasi*—a white lace overdress that came to her knees, partially covering a pair of long white linen pants. A lace belt encircled her ample waist and a large cameo pinned the bertha collar at her throat. A flat white hat with a red flower on the brim was perched on her head. Thayer hardly recognized Tofilau in his best dark suit with a white shirt and tie.

When they arrived at the church, they were promptly escorted to the front pew, where they found Von and Mrs. von Kuhrt already seated. Thayer nodded to Von and slipped in beside his mother, who patted her hand and whispered a greeting, "I'm so glad I felt able to come today, especially since I couldn't go to his funeral."

"I'm glad too," Thayer whispered back. Somehow the service would be more meaningful with the older woman there, for she had never spoken a word against Wilbur Elwood.

"Church means so much to Samoans," Mrs. von Kuhrt explained in a low voice. "And they live their religion too. They're true Christians."

As Thayer heard the congregation singing the hymns with such sincerity and watched the rapt attention they gave to the pastor, she had to agree.

For the memorial service the usher placed chairs across the front of the church for the *matai* and the lesser chiefs. The pastor spoke first and then the man

83

next to the *matai* took over the pulpit. Mrs. von Kuhrt explained in a whisper, "That's the talking chief who makes all the speeches."

As the talking chief listed all of Wilbur Elwood's virtues and accomplishments, as well as the kindnesses that he had shown to his employees and other Samoans, Thayer wanted to lean across and poke Von. If she could only say, "Hear that? Now what did you have to say about Uncle Wilbur?" The sincere and moving praise only reinforced Thayer's belief that her uncle's financial plight was all due to Von's deception.

When the memorial services were over and the congregation moved outside, Thayer thanked the chief, the pastor, and the talking chief.

The old *matai* said to her, "Next Saturday afternoon we will hold a kava ceremony in your honor so everyone can meet you. You will come to the meetinghouse at four o'clock."

He turned away to speak to Von, taking it for granted that she would be there, as, of course, she would be. How kind these Samoans were and how ready they were to make her part of their lives.

The next week things went surprisingly smoothly for Thayer at the orchid greenhouse. Taligi was very knowledgeable about the everyday routine of the business and there were no crises such as an outbreak of a disease. Mrs. von Kuhrt came for a while every day and they spent many happy hours together.

Thursday evening Russell telephoned. "Hello, Thayer! I'm coming on the interisland launch tomorrow. How about if I bring your paint, curtains, and upholstery material? The store has your order all ready and will deliver it to the boat in the morning."

"Marvelous!" Thayer exclaimed, astonished at how glad she was to hear his voice again. "I'll have Tofilau, my housekeeper's husband, meet the launch with the pickup and he can get the order."

"Fine. I know Tofilau. I'll ride with him across the island and he can drop me off at Hibiscus Lagoon. I'll see you there."

"But plan to have dinner with me tomorrow night at Seacrest. Bring your trunks so we can swim first."

"Great. I'll do that."

To work the next morning Thayer wore her most becoming pants and a top in a soft rose color. She brushed her freshly shampooed hair until it shone. All during the day she thought about Russell and waited for him impatiently.

She told Mrs. von Kuhrt about the kava ceremony planned for the next day. "Perhaps Russell would like to go with me."

"He might. But he usually spends the day going to the various plantations to advise the growers on their problems. In any case, would you like to come here after the kava ceremony and stay for dinner with us? We're not going to give Russell up for two evenings in a row."

The color rose in Thayer's cheeks. "Of course not. I'll come here instead."

Russell arrived in the middle of the afternoon. When he stepped into the greenhouse, his bright hair, his wide smile, and his kindly eyes seemed to bring a glow. "Hi, Thayer. Hard at it, I see."

She put down the pot of orchids she was carrying. "Russell. How good to see you!"

He looked her up and down, his eyes showing his admiration. "It's great seeing you like this, Thayer. Here you are with a good job and you're fixing up your house. Quite a change from the forlorn girl I saw at Pago Pago a couple of weeks ago."

"I hit bottom then. You were so kind to me and I'll

always be grateful. And now you've been my shopper."
She smiled up at him. "I can hardly wait to see everything!"

"I sent Tofilau on to Seacrest with them."

"It'll take a month's wages to pay the bill but it will
be worth it."

Russell looked around. "How are things going here?"

"So far, better than I dared hope. But the test will
come next week when I have to send out a shipment. I
really dread that."

"Once you do it, it'll be routine."

She showed him through the greenhouse and asked
his advice on several matters. Then he excused himself,
"I promised Von I'd check out a problem here with his
foreman. I'll see you later at Seacrest."

By the time Thayer got home, Tofilau had already
painted a portion of the wall in the living room for her
to see.

"I like it. It's going to be fine," Thayer said enthusiastically, and then opened the upholstery material.
They draped it over one of the chairs and they all exclaimed with admiration.

As she felt the material Fetu said, "It *is* beautiful. If
only Mr. Elwood could see this place when we get it
finished," she said wistfully.

Thayer swallowed the lump in her throat and went
on quickly. "We'll start tomorrow. We don't have to be
at the kava ceremony until four o'clock."

Russell arrived early so they had a chance to swim
before dinner. She felt almost shy in her brief bikini; he
couldn't seem to take his eyes away from her. His own
body was tall and muscular, his chest covered with
thick, curly red hair. He cut gracefully through the
water with long strong arms.

When they sat at the dinner table later, after they'd
showered and dressed, Thayer thought that someday,

when she chose a husband, he would be someone kind and thoughtful like Russell. Someone with whom she could feel completely relaxed and not tense and on edge.

They ate lobster salad, then Fetu served chicken pie with a flaky crust and baked yams and creamed peas. A rich chocolate cake and coffee finished the meal. It was surprising how much they found to talk about.

When the meal was over, they walked back to the beach and watched the moonlight dance on the rippling water. Finally Thayer began, "Russell, there's something I want to ask you and I want an honest answer. I get the impression that there was something wrong with Uncle Wilbur. Everyone implies so much, but they are holding back information. What is it?"

Russell hesitated and then said, "Frankly Wilbur was a heavy drinker. I've been here sometimes when he was completely out of it."

"Maybe you'd turn to drink too if you saw your life's work going down the drain." There was a defensive note in her voice.

"There was a lot he could have done to solve his problems around here if he'd left the booze alone."

"Not when he had powerful people working against him all the time."

"If you mean Von—"

"I do mean Von! He was—"

Russell stopped walking and put his hands on her shoulders. Facing her, he said, "I'm not going to get in an argument about Von. He's one of my closest friends and I'm afraid I'm completely prejudiced in his favor. I don't have the facts about your uncle's affairs so I'm not going to discuss them. I just saw him in bad shape several times. That's all I know."

"Poor Uncle Wilbur." She turned her head away. "Thanks anyway, Russ."

"Let's forget Uncle Wilbur, Thayer, and talk about us." He slipped his arm around her waist. "You're so beautiful. I've been counting the days to be with you. This could be just the beginning for us."

"Yes, just the beginning," she echoed.

CHAPTER 9

The next afternoon when Thayer joined Fetu and Tofilau to go to the kava ceremony, she noticed that the
housekeeper carried a large cake.

"Was I suppose to bring something?" Thayer asked.

"No, this is for the feast afterward."

Thayer's heart sank. "Oh, dear, I accepted an invitation to Mrs. von Kuhrt's for dinner."

Fetu smiled. "You're not expected to stay. You can
if you want but you don't have to." She handed Thayer
the cake to hold while she settled her bulk in the backseat of the VW. Then, when she had the cake safely
placed on her lap, she went on. "The chief is having the
kava ceremony to honor you and give everyone a
chance to meet you. Then you can leave if you want.
We'll all play bingo for a couple of hours before we
have the feast."

"Bingo?" Thayer smiled to herself as she climbed in
next to Tofilau, who was behind the wheel; somehow
the last thing she expected these Polynesians to play
was bingo. But why not? How stereotyped was her idea
of them before she left the States. Somehow she visual-
ized them dancing on the beach all the time, but of
course they didn't. They had to earn a living, raise their
families, cook, and clean house just like everyone else
in the world.

Nearly two hundred adults were gathered outside the
meetinghouse, to say nothing of the dozens of children
who shouted and chased each other in the meadow.
Fetu held back until the *matai* officially welcomed

Thayer, then she bustled around importantly, introducing her to all the Samoans.

"They've come from all the plantations around here to meet you," Fetu said at one point.

Finally the *matai* led the way into the meetinghouse, a large oval-shaped *fale* without walls, with a thatched roof supported by posts all around the edge. Thick leaves and flowers covered every post, and garlands of hibiscus formed a canopy of honor at one end. Thayer was startled to see Von sitting cross-legged on a pandanus mat under the canopy.

The *matai* waved his arm, indicating that she was to sit next to Von, then he himself sat against the largest and most elaborately decorated post. The lesser chiefs arranged themselves according to rank at the other posts. Thayer noticed that they were fully tattooed from their waists to their knees.

Thayer leaned to Von and whispered, "What are you doing here?"

"I'm an honorary chief here on Nanotuma. Today I get the privilege of sitting next to you, the guest of honor."

As many people as possible crowded into the meetinghouse and sat in a circle on the pandanus mats that covered the pebbled floor. The others stood outside to watch. When they were all quiet, a man pounded on a hollow drum and a handsome young man appeared with a long gnarled stick scraped white, which he handed to the *matai*.

Then a beautiful young girl, wearing a crown of flowers and a blue sarong, entered the meetinghouse accompanied by two young men. As the hollow drum thundered they crossed the room and seated themselves behind a four-legged wooden bowl.

"That's the *matai*'s virgin granddaughter," Von whispered. "She's the Village Maiden."

90

One of the young men shook a leaf of pounded kava root into the bowl while the other ladled in water with half a coconut shell. Gracefully the girl kneaded and squeezed the liquid with a roll of fiber. At intervals she tossed the fiber strainer to a young man outside who shook it out and tossed it back.

Gradually the liquid turned brown. The Village Maiden then held up the strainer and let the fluid drip back into the bowl. The chiefs all nodded their approval and the *matai* smiled at his granddaughter and indicated that she had made well the ancient ceremonial drink of Samoa.

Fascinated, Thayer watched the ancient ritual that had been used for special occasions throughout the centuries and felt almost overwhelmed with gratitude that these kindly people would do it for her.

The chiefs clapped hands, then one let out a fearsome shout followed by a volley of words. One of the male attendants jumped up, dipped a coconut shell into the kava, lifted it above his head, and strode to the middle of the room. The chief shouted again and the man turned slowly and with a sweep of his arm handed it to the village pastor. Thayer as guest of honor was served next. She forced herself to swallow the strange fluid.

The talking chief, speech-maker and authority on protocol, took the coconut shell from her, poured a drop to the gods, and drank, tossing the dregs over his shoulder. The attendant then served each chief according to rank.

While the chiefs and other important men were being served, the Village Maiden stepped outside. Finally one of the chiefs shouted again and the men all began to chant. The Village Maiden came into the meetinghouse again, carrying a mat.

One at a time the girls swept their mats gracefully around the circle before the guests. The mats had been woven with infinite patience from pandanus leaves split fine as threads. One of the mats was bordered with soft red feathers. After the mats were admired by all, they were presented to Thayer. She gasped with disbelief that she was to have anything so exquisite.

She started to get to her feet to thank the guests when Von pulled her back, whispering, "The talking chief is the only one who makes speeches. He'll thank everyone for you."

For half an hour the talking chief, dressed in a short lavalava that displayed his tattooed thighs, spoke in Samoan. As one pointed to Thayer and Von, the guests laughed, clapped, and cheered. A smile twitched Von's lips.

Finally it was all over. Fetu held the mats while Thayer went around and thanked as many people as she could.

Von took the mats from Fetu and said, "You might as well ride over to Hibiscus Lagoon with me. I understand you're coming for dinner. I'm sure Russell will be happy to take you home later."

On the way he asked, "What did you think of the kava ceremony?"

"It was very impressive. Really wonderful. I can't get over the fact that they would put it on for me. And I feel terrible about taking these beautiful mats. Each one represents weeks of work. Those people hardly know me."

"Well, of course, they consider that you've taken Wilbur's place in their community, but I must say that you've completely won their hearts."

"What was the talking chief saying when he pointed at us and everyone laughed and cheered?" she asked.

"I was afraid you'd ask me that." He smiled again. "I don't think I'll tell you."

"Now I'm curious. I insist on knowing."

"No. It's better left unsaid."

Exasperated, she tried to think of a rejoiner to cut him down to size, but all she could manage was "Tell me. It's not polite to discuss someone in a foreign language that she can't understand."

"You're right there. But you won't like it."

"Try me."

He glanced at her, amusement dancing in his eyes, which annoyed her beyond endurance. "Well, here goes. The talking chief said that the gods sent you here because I needed a wife. Someone young, beautiful, and charming who would make a good mistress at Hibiscus Lagoon and bear many children for me."

"What!" She stared at him in astonishment before embarrassment turned her cheeks pink. Then she said tersely, "I can't imagine anything less likely to happen."

"Neither can I. But it is funny, isn't it?"

"If we can go on as employer and employee, we'll be doing well," Thayer said, thankful that they were entering Hibiscus Lagoon.

"I'd say that Russell is more your type."

"I couldn't agree with you more!" She jumped out of the car as soon as it stopped at the side entrance.

Von reached in the backseat for the mats and handed them to her muttering, "You are young, beautiful, and charming, but *what* a disposition."

She grabbed the mats from him. "The gods didn't send me here; I came on my own. And someday I intend to leave the same way."

Feeling flustered and more than a little shaken, she rang the doorbell. When a maid admitted her, she marched through the house to the terrace, where she found Russell and Mrs. von Kuhrt.

After she greeted them, she said, "Look what the villagers gave me! These belong in a museum. I have no

93

right to them." She spread her mats out on the terrace for them to see and admire.

As Mrs. von Kuhrt felt their suppleness, she said, "Don't worry about them. Enjoy them while you can. They are ceremonial gift mats. You'll have plenty of occasions to pass them on when some village girl gets married. They've been used over and over as gifts, and one sends them on to someone else at the appropriate time."

"I feel better, then." She sat down next to Russell, grateful for his nearness and the relaxed feeling he gave her.

Soon the lord of the manor arrived and fixed drinks for them all. Later, after dinner, they played bridge, and, as luck would have it, Thayer drew Von for a partner. It was hard to keep her mind on the game as she kept remembering the talking chief's prediction. Too, Von's skill made her feel inept. She was grateful when Mrs. von Kuhrt announced that she'd had enough.

On the way home Russell put his arm around her and she leaned against him. Then he said, "I'm afraid I won't see you tomorrow. I'm going to help Von in the morning and I'm attending a special meeting of growers at the other end of the island in the afternoon and flying back to Pago Pago with one of them in his private plane afterward."

"I'm sorry. I've enjoyed seeing you."

"Thayer, there's going to be a big Fourth of July celebration in Pago Pago. Would you come over for the weekend? I have a friend, a girl I want you to meet, who lives with her family there, and I know she'll put you up. She's engaged to a guy in my office."

"I'd love to, Russ. I can come on the launch."

"No, Von is coming too. He's flying over. I've already arranged a ride for you."

94

She would have much preferred the launch but she said nothing. It was all two weeks away and Von could very well change his mind. In the meantime she had something wonderful to look forward to.

When they arrived at Seacrest, they stopped alongside the house and looked out at the bay, silvered again by the lopsided moon. They could hear the waves lap against the sand and the palm trees rustle in the darkness. A night bird called as it fluttered from one tree to the next. Overhead the sky was burning with stars that were big and close against their background of deep and infinite indigo.

Thayer said, "You were right when you said I would get hooked on Samoa. I am already."

"It's paradise, all right." He touched her hair and then drew her to him. "It's been wonderful seeing you again." He kissed her, then said, "It would be so easy to fall in love with you. You're so beautiful. So lovely."

How gentle and sweet Russell was. He didn't grab her and kiss her with savagery the way Von had done. He brought out the very best in her—a ladylike refinement—instead of appealing to her baser side. As Von himself had said, Russ was more her type.

Finally she drew away from him. "You'd better go back to Hibiscus Lagoon. Von will be wondering where you are." She didn't want to give her employer any more reason for criticism.

Before he left, Russell kissed her again, and she went into the house feeling a little disturbed. The next day she'd be entirely alone and she was glad that Fetu and her husband were going to visit relatives. She needed a chance to sort out her muddled feelings. She'd start to sew the cushion covers, a routine task, and take time to think.

Before she climbed into bed, she looked out at the sea again and watched the moonlight on the water. But her thoughts turned to Von. Her cheeks flushed again as she thought of the talking chief's prediction that she had been sent by the gods as a wife for Von. And she was to produce many children for him. How embarrassing. Now the whole village would conjecture and gossip about them.

The first part of the week was a busy one. At work there were plants to select and prepare for shipping. She wished Alefosio would happen to drop in so she could ask him a question or two. But she wouldn't send for him; she had managed so far and she was determined to carry through. Every time Von appeared on the scene, the nerves in her stomach tensed into a ball.

At least in the evenings she could relax as she sewed her cushion covers. Fortunately she had helped her mother, who was an excellent seamstress, refurbish their sunroom at home so Thayer knew how to tackle this job. Fetu helped too, so the undertaking moved along. Tofilau, with much prodding from his wife, spent his days painting the woodwork and the walls.

On Wednesday evening, while she was sewing in the study, she heard a car drive up. Fetu's dog barked, and soon the front doorbell rang. When she answered it, she found Von at the entrance.

"Well, hello. Come on in," she said, stepping aside, "but be careful of the fresh paint."

He handed a package to her. "Our housekeeper had borrowed these things from Fetu. She wanted to return them, and since I was going by here tonight, I offered to bring them."

She took the package and put it on the dining room table. "We're redecorating. Won't you come and see?"

She led him into the living room, where the woodwork and shutters were freshly painted white and three of the walls were already pale green. The remaining wall, still streaked and dirty, showed what they had accomplished.

Von looked around. "It's beautiful. I had no idea it could look so nice. It's been so long since anything was done around here."

She was annoyed with herself for being so inordinately pleased with his approval. What difference did it make what he thought? This was her house, wasn't it?

But she went on. "We're going to relacquer all this rattan furniture, which is of excellent quality. Then Fetu and I are making new covers for all the cushions. I'm sewing here in the study. Come see the material."

When she held up a finished cushion, Von nodded his approval. "It's great." He looked at her strangely. "There's no limit to your talents."

"I'm going to use lots of plants in the living room. Especially ferns. And I hope you'll let me buy some of your orchids, Cypripedium Christine and Cymbidium Jocosity. That will repeat the green and gold."

"Take them with my compliments as a housewarming gift from Mother and me. I had no idea that you were such a nest-builder."

"Well, thank you. I'm so anxious for your mother to see all this when we're through. You'll have to bring her over for dinner then."

The bill for her order lay on the top of the package of panel curtains. To her horror he picked it up, looked at the total, and whistled. "Good Lord."

As she grabbed the bill from him she felt herself stiffen and a pulse began to hammer in her temple. Her temper flared white-hot. "It's not being charged to the plantation, if that's what you're worrying about!" she said angrily. "I'm paying for it out of my salary, so it's none of your business how much it costs."

"I apologize for looking at the bill. It is none of my business, I admit."

Her chin trembled. "You're the chief honcho around here and think you can get by with anything. Just remember this is *my* house and what I do to it is entirely *my* affair. Not yours."

His eyes glittered dangerously, and his mouth made a thin line. "I just hope that we can keep the plantation afloat so that you can stay here at Seacrest and enjoy all your work and expenditure in *your* house."

Her eyes encountered his directly, and they stared at each other unthinkingly, exploring, until a look of bafflement replaced his fury. For a moment they glimpsed something strange and bewildering in each other, then the moment passed.

Finally she twisted herself away from him. "Would you please go."

He left without a word. She sat down at the sewing machine and pedaled furiously, trying to work off her anger and chagrin at Von. And herself too. What had he read in her eyes? He had made her absolutely livid, yet she had wanted him to take her in his arms. Was she out of her mind? This appeal they had for each other, these pure primitive emotions, were not controlled by reason.

The next morning as she went to the office to sign up for the panel truck and get the keys, she ran into Von first thing. There he was, of course, right in the outer office.

"You're shipping plants today, aren't you?" he asked.

"Yes." She averted his gaze.

"Do you have them all ready?"

"Of course I do."

He followed her outside. "Don't you think I'd better go with you this first time?"

"No, I don't! I can handle it."

98

"Don't forget the bill of lading."

"I won't."

"Be sure and get them to the freighter in plenty of time. The captain doesn't wait for anyone. He sails promptly at two."

"I'll take care of it," she said coldly.

With her head high in the air, she marched to the garage, found her truck, and backed it out of its stall. " 'Don't forget the bill of lading.' 'Be sure and get them to the freighter in plenty of time,' " she mocked aloud as she drove the truck to the greenhouse.

It seemed to take them forever to load the truck. Things went much faster when Alefosio was in charge. Why was that? The longer it took, the more nervous she got. Finally she was ready. She drove out of the plantation, and followed the main road toward Falelumu. Nervously she watched for her landmarks and felt better when she recognized one. It was taking much longer than she'd expected.

As she drove up in the grade through the rain forest the truck began to sputter. Although she stepped hard on the accelerator to urge it along, the truck was moving slower and slower. She urged the truck to the edge of the road, where it came to a complete stop.

CHAPTER 10

"What's wrong?" Thayer said aloud as she pumped on the gas pedal, then turned the key in the starter. But the engine was dead.

Then she looked at the gas gauge and her heart sank like a lead ball. She'd forgotten to fill the tank, which registered empty. It was all her own fault, just a dumb, careless mistake on her part.

She remembered how Von had followed her outside giving her instructions. "Don't forget the bill of lading." "Be sure and get them to the freighter in plenty of time." If he'd minded his own business, she'd have remembered the gas. Now what was she going to do?

She glanced at her wristwatch. It was noon. The freighter sailed at two o'clock. She had to get her orchid plants to the dock long before that. What a predicament. Why did this have to happen on her first shipping day? How could she explain this to Von? Finally she climbed out of the truck and walked up and down the road. There was no one in sight. If she'd only realized her situation sooner, she could have stopped at a plantation along the way.

She tried to think what she should do. Should she walk back down the grade? How far was it? The sun beat down on her unmercifully. She felt her thin top become damp and sticky.

Her first shipping day and she forgot to get gas in the truck. Now it seemed impossible that she could have been so careless. If only she'd have let Von come with her this first time. He was quite sincere in his offer, she had to admit, but she'd been so know-it-all. Now look what a spot she was in.

By twelve thirty she was in tears. She assumed that everyone was at the dock. Pretty soon it would be too late. Finally, about one o'clock, she heard a truck come laboring up the grade from the other side. When it came over the summit, she stood out in the center of the road and waved her arms.

The ancient Ford pickup stopped in front of her and an old Samoan stuck his head out of the side. She ran up to him and shouted above the noise of his engine, "I'm out of gas. Could you possibly help me? I have a load for the freighter and I must get it there."

A volley of Samoa words poured out of his wrinkled face. He grinned toothlessly and shook his head, and it was evident that he couldn't speak English.

She gestured and shoved to show that she wanted him to push her truck. He looked around, shook his head again, and drove past. Helplessly she watched him go.

But soon she saw that he'd only been hunting a wider place in the road to turn around. He maneuvered his old truck around and came toward her, grinning and waving her back in her own vehicle. She jumped behind the wheel just in time to release the brake before he shoved against the bumper.

Slowly they pushed up the grade, and she hoped his old truck would have power enough to get them both to the summit. Finally they made it and she went coasting down the mountain around the hairpin turns. She prayed that the old man would stay with her. She glanced in the mirror and he was behind. Finally they reached the bottom, and he pushed her along until they came to a rusty gas pump in front of a grocery store in the port.

She jumped out, took a five-dollar bill out of her

purse, and ran back to him. "Thank you. *Fa'afetai!*" She dropped the bill on the seat beside him and waved as he drove happily away.

A young boy about ten came out of the store and took the gas nozzle out of the pump. She held up one hand. "Do you want five gallon?" the boy asked in English.

"That's right. As fast as you can."

By the time she got to the dock it was nearly two o'clock. She found a stevedore with a hand truck and frantically helped him unload some of her boxes. Then she ran up the gangplank with her bill of lading.

A big burly officer shook his head. "It's too late. I—"

"It's not too late. I have a shipment of orchid plants and they have to go! And I must have a cool place for them too." She waved to the stevedore. "Come on."

Soon a bearded, weather-wrinkled captain appeared. "What's the trouble?"

Thayer looked at him and saw the faintest glint of compassion in his eyes. "Oh, please, I have a shipment of orchid plants from Hibiscus Lagoon. They must go today! They must be in a cool place and where they can be sprayed too."

"What happened to Alefosio? He always got them here in the morning, instead of just as we're ready to pull anchor."

"He's been made manager of one of the Von Kuhrt plantations. Now I'm in charge of the orchid greenhouse at Hibiscus Lagoon and I've had an awful time getting here! I ran out of gas. If you'll just show me—" Tears glinted in her eyes as she looked pleadingly at the captain. Silently she prayed for his consent.

Amusement showed in his gruff expression. "All right. Come along, miss, if you insist. Higgins, get some men to unload that panel truck in a hurry. They're to step lively too."

Thayer supervised the placing of the plants in the hold, got her copy of the bill of lading signed, and said to the captain and other crew members gathered around, "You'll take care of them, won't you? I'm going to telephone the broker in Auckland when you get there to see what condition they're in."

"Oh, you are, are you?" the captain answered trying to hide a smile. But he shook hands with her. "I promise to do our best. Now if you'll kindly go ashore, we'll get underway. We're already twenty minutes late. Mind you don't do this to me again."

"I won't. I promise. Thank you so much."

She ran down the gangplank, waved good-bye from the dock, and then turned to pay the stevedores, her knees shaking with relief.

As she drove back to Hibiscus Lagoon she decided to turn in to the office only the amount that Alefosio had paid the stevedore two weeks before so Von would never know what happened. The whole incident had cost her an extra fifteen dollars, rather an expensive lesson, she thought ruefully. But at least Von would never know, which was the most important thing.

When she turned in the truck keys and bill of lading, then filled out the expense form in the office, she was relieved that her boss was not around. She couldn't face his probing eyes and direct questions. He'd put her through a third degree until he knew everything. Evasively she said to the girl. "I'm sure the plants will arrive in good shape. The captain promised me that they'd take care of them."

Even when she saw Von the next day, nothing was said about the shipment, and she felt she'd gotten through that crisis better than she deserved.

Now she could turn her attention to getting Mrs. von Kuhrt started on a challenging project. When the older woman arrived at the greenhouse, Thayer asked, "How

103

would you like to learn about hand pollination? Between orchids of the same kind, of course. It would be enormously helpful here and be the first step before we try any hybridizing or try developing new varieties."

"I'd love to learn," Mrs. von Kuhrt said, her eyes alive with interest. "Tell me about it."

"You and I could pollinate an orchid in an instant, but as you know in nature it's a very complicated process when the insects carry pollen from one plant to the other."

"I suppose it is."

"Orchids are equipped with an ingenious mechanism for pollination that will only work if an insect of just the right size and shape comes to it. A tiny orchid requires a very small insect, while a large orchid might need a moth with a long proboscis to pollinate it. A flower can be visited by lots of insects, yet it may wither and die before the right one comes along. When it does, believe it or not, the orchid literally glues the parcel of pollen to the insect's anatomy."

Thayer then showed Mrs. von Kuhrt how to remove the anther of an orchid onto a clean piece of paper and then nudge the waxy mass of pollen grains out of the anther. Thayer took a clean toothpick, touched the tip of the sticky fluid of the stigma, then picked up the pollen mass and placed it on the stigma of another orchid where it would develop into a seed pod.

As they worked Thayer said, "I'm going to have a special table built for you that will fit right over your wheelchair. Then you can work without leaning forward. That's too tiring for you."

"Indeed it is!" Von spoke from the doorway. "What on earth are you doing, Mother?" He walked over to them.

"I'm learning to pollinate orchids."

Thayer was acutely aware of his height, his broad shoulders, and the muscles that rippled under his light shirt. She put her equipment down and said, "Your mother's going to become an orchidist. There's no reason why she can't learn all about them. Later she's going to start hybridizing and develop a whole line of Von Kuhrt orchids."

Mrs. von Kuhrt looked up at her son. "You know how I've always longed to be part of this operation. Now, for the first time, I can be. Thayer makes me feel so welcome, I'll have a whole new interest in life."

"But, Mother, are you up to working in this greenhouse? Won't you get too tired? I question——"

Thayer interupted, "Oh, come off of it! Your mother and I have some common sense. We're quite capable of deciding when she gets too tired. And when she is, I'll take her back to the house."

"Make sure that you do. I don't want her to have a setback."

Thayer turned to the older woman and said, "I'm in charge here and I'm going to see to it that you learn all about raising orchids, that you become an expert orchidist. We can go to orchid shows and exhibit and do all kinds of interesting things with our plants."

"Good for you." Mrs. von Kuhrt plainly showed her amusement.

Thayer went on. "I'll manage. I'll take care of everything."

For a long moment Von looked at her searchingly. She couldn't read the inscrutable expression on his face. Was he angry?

Finally he burst out, "You'll manage all right! I don't doubt that for a moment. Anyone who could get old Paulo, who doesn't speak a word of English, to push her truck to the gas pump and who can persuade a hard-nosed captain to delay sailing can do anything!"

As he turned and left, Thayer called after him, "Apparently you have spies everywhere, Mr. von Kuhrt."

"I do. So watch it!" were his last words.

Mrs. von Kuhrt laughed. "Score one for Von! I think you're about even now."

"Oh, he drives me up the wall! Even if he is your son."

"Anyway, you won't pull any wool over his eyes, Thayer, so don't try to. And I'm surprised that he takes so much from you. No one else ever challenges him the way you do. As I said before, he's the undisputed boss at Hibiscus Lagoon, except here in the orchid house."

"Well, he makes me furious. And he'd better not try being boss here. I won't stand for it."

They worked together until lunchtime. After a maid came for Mrs. von Kuhrt, Thayer sat in the shade, and as she ate her sandwich she thought about Von. So he'd known all about her misadventure of running out of gas the day before. She hadn't fooled him a bit. But why hadn't he said something?

All weekend she worked with Fetu and Tofilau until the redecorating project was finally finished. As they stood in the living room, admiring their work late Sunday afternoon, they heard a car drive up, and soon Von, Mrs. von Kuhrt, and Tupuasa were at the front door.

"We just had to come see what you've done here!" Mrs. von Kuhrt exclaimed as Von pushed her wheelchair in the front door. She looked around. "It's beautiful! How effective those pale green walls are. It looks so cool and refreshing in here. And those new cushions look as if they'd been professionally done. What a clever girl you are, Thayer!"

106

"Fetu sewed on them too. And Tofilau did all the painting," Thayer said as the two Samoans beamed with pleasure at her praise.

Von patted the older man on the shoulder. "You did a great job. I never expected the place to look like this."

"Well, we never had anyone like Miss Elwood around here before."

Von threw back his head and laughed. "You can say that again. Hibiscus Lagoon isn't the same either. It's like having a typhoon hit there."

The color rose in Thayer's cheeks. Why would he make a remark like that? Was she really such a disturbing element? "You're our first guests so please sit down. Let's have tea or a drink or something."

Fetu said, "I'll bring some refreshments right away."

The Samoans disappeared in the kitchen, and Von said, "I brought the orchids you wanted and some ferns as a housewarming gift from Mother, Tupuasa, and me."

"Oh, how marvelous! I can't thank you enough." Thayer ran across the room to where Mrs. von Kuhrt had seated herself and kissed her. Then she turned to Von, her eyes sparkling with pleasure. "I'll come out to the car and help you carry them in."

When Von opened the trunk of his car, she gasped with delight at the lovely orchids and ferns that would add the final touch to her living room. She looked up at him, "You can be so nice and thoughtful. You can't imagine how much pleasure these will bring me. I don't—" *What a complex, compelling man you are,* she thought. The way his eyes narrowed and pinned her, like now, drawing her to him with his own kind of black magic, until she forgot what she was going to say.

"If my mother deserved a thank-you kiss, don't I?"

107

And his lips were on hers, and a ripple of longing for him ran through her.

Confused, almost frightened by the intensity of her response, she broke away and picked up one of the orchid pots and carried it into the house.

They had tea, a long visit, and Fetu even managed a simple dinner for everyone later. All the time she felt at a fever-pitch, exhilarated, as if a new dimension had been added to her life. When her guests left at ten o'clock, Thayer went into the study, too restless to go upstairs to bed. She remembered the arrogant tilt to his head, the expressions that changed his handsome, aristocratic face; some were serious, some amused, some thoughtful. She could still feel the touch of Von's hand on her arm as he said good-bye.

Then she recalled her uncle's letter: "But the main reason I'm here is to get advice on how to fight my neighbor, Eiland von Kuhrt. He's trying to get everything away from me. He's nothing but a thief. . . ."

Why did Uncle Wilbur feel that way? Obviously there had been genuine devotion between the older Von Kuhrts and Wilbur; they had been neighbors and friends for years. Since Von's mother had been so grieved by Wilbur's death, there couldn't have been animosity. What had happened to cause such bitterness between her uncle and Von?

For the first time she considered the possibility that perhaps Wilbur had been completely mistaken. Why would Von steal his plantation and workers when he had so many successful plantations already? When he was one of the wealthiest planters in Samoa, the accusation was ridiculous. Von could buy anything he wanted; he didn't have to steal from Wilbur.

She opened one of the filing cabinet drawers and found a divider marked SEACREST. It surprised her to see a stiff manila folder with IMPORTANT EVIDENCE written across it, overflowing with papers. She pulled the folder out and opened it on the desk.

As she looked through the papers, reports, invoices, and letters, a wave of revulsion sickened her. Uncle Wilbur was right. There was no question about it. Von was deliberately gaining control of Seacrest . . . stealing everything.

CHAPTER 11

The next morning Thayer tried to be her usual cheerful self with Mrs. von Kuhrt, despite the leaden ache near her heart. She arranged materials and orchid plants so the two of them could go on with the hand pollination project. Too she called in the plantation carpenter to measure the wheelchair and design a special worktable to fit over it.

But all morning Mrs. von Kuhrt seemed blue and depressed too. Finally, when they were alone, the older woman looked at her with tears swimming in her eyes. "Von told me this morning that he has invited Lisa Campbell to come for a long visit. I think he's going to marry her."

An unexpected wrench jolted Thayer. "Who is Lisa Campbell?"

"She is the daughter of a planter in Western Samoa. They're from an old New Zealand family and they spend part of the year in Christ Church. I know them all. They're prominent and well-established. Lisa has been well brought up and is an accomplished musician. She is suitable, all right. It's just that I can't stand her." Her chin quivered as she wiped her eyes with a tissue.

Thayer put her arm across Mrs. von Kuhrt's shoulders. "Oh, I'm so sorry."

"Lisa's going to be with Von in Pago Pago for the Fourth of July weekend and is then coming here for the rest of the month. I'm certain they'll announce their engagement. I know it. It just breaks my heart."

110

"But as you're around Lisa you may learn to like her. Perhaps you've misunderstood her."

"Oh, no. I know her too well. That's the trouble. She's beautiful, spoiled, and shallow. She won't make Von a good wife at all."

"I can imagine why you're so upset." Her own throat tightened with pity for Von's mother, and there was another subtle feeling of despair as well. Why would such news bother her at all? Surely it wouldn't affect her job.

"You'll soon see what I mean. She's all sweetness and honey in front of Von but horrid to me behind his back. She always make cutting remarks to me." She put her hands over her face and started to cry. "How can I ever live here with Lisa?"

While her own eyes swam with tears, Thayer held Mrs. von Kuhrt close. What a shame that a person as sweet and superior as Von's mother had to suffer over this development.

"Would you like to have me take you back to the house? You're too upset to do much today."

"Yes, I'm just sick about this. I'll have to go to bed."

In the days that followed, Mrs. von Kuhrt never mentioned Lisa Campbell again. It was as if she were too heartsick to discuss the subject. How could Von do this to his mother when it was obvious that he was so devoted to her? But then look what he had done to her uncle. She didn't know Von; he might be capable of anything.

Thayer decided that the kindest thing was to get Mrs. von Kuhrt even more deeply involved in orchid culture. Together they made a study of the insects and mites that attack orchids. They learned which species were affected by special flies and weevils and that all orchids could be hosts to insects. They learned how to control mites, thrips, and aphids and studied such diseases as

111

black rot, leaf rust, and leaf spot. The more they learned, the more fascinated they became.

Frequently in the evening Russell would telephone and say, "It's just a few days until the Fourth of July. I can hardly wait. Everything's all set."

He told her that she would stay with Judy Rhinehart's family from Sydney, who would be delighted to have Thayer as a guest. Mr. Rhinehart was manager of an Australian import-export company where Judy worked as a secretary. Judy was engaged to Mike Snyder who worked in Russell's office, so naturally the four of them would attend all the functions together.

"I'm wondering about clothes. Will I need anything for evening?"

"Yes. We're going to a dance at the Samoan Inn. But otherwise it's very casual."

After she replaced the receiver, she sat at Wilbur's desk and thought about Russell and how she looked forward to seeing him again. Ever since she had discovered the folder of evidence against Von, she longed even more for the comfort of Russell's concern and kindness.

On the afternoon of the third she quit work early, showered, and dressed at Hibiscus Lagoon and was ready with her luggage when Von appeared, immaculate and handsome in his tropical slacks and shirt. They both kissed Mrs. von Kuhrt good-bye before they climbed in the Land-Rover and drove to Von's private airplane.

As the craft flew over the blue water Thayer thought of all the things that had happened in the short time she'd been in Samoa. Already it had woven its spell around her and felt like home. It was hard to believe that she had been so frightened and lost the last time she had flown from Pago Pago to Nanotuma with no job, little money, and no idea where to turn. If it hadn't

112

have been for her discovery of evidence of Von's guilt, how perfect her life would be now.

Suddenly she was aware that Von was looking at her appreciatively. She wore a white cotton crepe dress with a drawstring around her slender waist. A pink shell necklace and bracelet gave the only spot of color. White canvas espadrilles on her bare feet and a white straw bag completed her outfit.

"You look very attractive, Thayer," he said at last.

"Thank you, Von." In spite of everything she wanted his approval. Finally she went on. "I'm staying with the Rhineharts who are friends of Russell. Do you know them?"

"Of course. I often do business with Mr. Rhinehart. You'll have a ball with them." He adjusted the controls. "I'll be a guest of the governor and his wife. You must meet them. Lisa Campbell, a friend of mine, will be there too. By the way, she'll be coming back to Hibiscus Lagoon with us. You'll enjoy her."

"I'm sure I will. I'll have all of you for dinner while she's there."

"Fine. Lisa will appreciate that. We'll have you over to hear her play. She's a superb pianist. Has even played with the symphony in Christ Church."

They were silent awhile and then Von spoke again. "You've performed a miracle with Seacrest, Thayer. Mother and I can't get over it."

"I'm delighted with it too. I expect to settle down and live there a long time."

"I hope you do. And I want you to know that I think you are doing a great job with the orchid department. Mother's so interested in it. I appreciate your kindness to her."

"I just love your mother. She'll become a real expert with orchids. It's good for her to have that absorbing interest."

113

"I have to admit you're right. I didn't intend to make an invalid of her, but perhaps I have kept her from being as active as she should be. It's great you've encouraged that side of her."

Well, that was quite an admission from His Royal Highness, she thought. She never dreamed she'd hear him say that his actions were less than perfect.

When they arrived at the airport, Russell was there to meet them. He kissed Thayer, shook hands with Von, and they were soon on their way back to town. After they dropped off Von, they drove to a neat white house surrounded by a well-kept lawn and clipped hedges. An Indian mulberry tree and a Norfolk Island pine shaded the side veranda.

A pretty girl with wavy brown hair, a faint dusting of freckles across her nose, and a friendly smile met them at the front door. "Hi!"

Russell introduced them, and Judy slipped her hand under Thayer's arm. "Let's bring your things to my room. You'll have to share it with me because we have other houseguests." She laughed. "We're Australians but *everyone* in American Samoa celebrates the Fourth of July."

Thayer liked Judy instantly and realized how much she'd missed not having a girl friend her own age here in Samoa.

Soon Judy's fiancé arrived. He was a stocky, broad-shouldered American not much taller than Judy but as outgoing and likable as she was. They joined the other guests on the veranda for planter's punch before they ate a lamb curry dinner.

The next morning Russell and Mike called for the two girls to take them to the Independence Day parade. Part of the marching groups, such as the scout troops, veterans, and brass bands were *papalagi* or "white

114

man's way"; but Thayer was more interested in the *fa'a Samoa* sections that featured young, handsome men in lavalavas and attractive girls in tapa cloth costumes with bleached bark overshirts. As the American flag passed by she thought how strange it was to watch an international gathering in a faraway tropical island celebrate so earnestly America's independence from England so long ago.

At lunchtime they found a vendor who sold delicious *palusami,* thick coconut cream wrapped in a young taro leaf baked on hot stones and served on slices of cooked taro. Later they watched longboat races in which crews of nearly forty rowers pulled their *fautasi* through the ink-blue waters of the bay.

As she strolled hand-in-hand with Russell, Thayer had a glorious time. She felt the pressure of his strong fingers on her own and thought again of how easy it would be to fall in love with him. He was the epitome of kindness and honor, as well as a striking figure with his red-gold hair. It would be a privilege for any girl to have him as a husband.

How congenial the four of them were, she thought, and when they found a shady bench where they could sit down and have long, cool drinks, she asked Mike, "Do you plan to stay here after you're married?"

"Yes, I love it here. I never want to leave Samoa. I don't always want to be an agricultural adviser with the government, though."

Judy put in, "Someday he'd like to manage a plantation."

"I'm looking for a setup where I could manage a plantation on a salary with a percentage of the net profits," Mike explained. "That way I could build up some capital and later branch out on my own as a planter."

Thayer asked, "Have you talked to Eiland von

Kuhrt? He has several plantations on Nanotuma and other islands too. I believe he has such an arrangement with his managers."

"I know Von, of course. I've been on some of his properties but I've never brought this up to him."

Russell finished his drink. "You'll probably see Von at the dinner dance tonight. Maybe you'll have a chance to talk to him."

"He might be very busy with Lisa Campbell," Thayer said. "I understand that he's bringing her back to Hibiscus Lagoon for a visit."

Russell nodded. "They're quite a twosome. Lisa's a beautiful heiress and would be very suitable for Von."

Thayer thought of Von's mother but only said, "I've never met her. Perhaps I will tonight."

Tiredly Judy slumped against the back of the bench. "I know her. Frankly she's a pain in the neck. Von's much too nice a guy to get stuck with her."

Mike laughed and patted her hair. "Meow! Meow!"

"All right, so I'm catty. But I mean it. I do have to say though that she's one of the finest pianists I've ever heard." She stood up then. "Let's go home and get some rest before we shower and change for the dinner dance. I've had it."

Thayer stood up too. "I'm beat, that's for sure. I'm not quite used to this tropical climate yet. It gets to me."

That night Thayer, dressed in a long coral chiffon print, watched for Von and Lisa at the dinner dance. Finally she saw them come in the door, and a strange, sinking sensation washed over her. Lisa, in a white lace ball gown that contrasted with her tanned skin and long golden hair, was a sophisticated, breathtaking beauty. As all eyes turned to the handsome couple; they made an incredible picture in the doorway.

116

Judy poked her. "There she is, Miss Universe herself. She knows she's creating a sensation. But she's not my cup of tea. Just wait'll she gives you the shaft sometime, and you'll see what I mean."

"She'll have plenty of chance when she's visiting at Hibiscus Lagoon. You have me worried," Thayer said half seriously. What would it be like when Lisa became the mistress of the plantation? Well, she'd have to cross that bridge later.

As Lisa and Von passed their table they stopped, and introductions were made. Lisa looked her up and down as she said, "Von was saying that you were one of his newest employees."

Von put in quickly, "Fortunately for me, Thayer came at the right time to take that orchid project off my hands."

When they left, Judy turned to Thayer and giggled, "Crawl back under your rock, you lowly insect. Her Highness has spoken."

They all laughed, but Thayer could understand Mrs. von Kuhrt's apprehension.

As they ate their dinner, they admired the red, white, and blue decorations. Later, when the orchestra began to play, Thayer floated in Russell's arms, as he was an excellent dancer. Not only that, he was a marvelous person in every way, she decided.

Once, when Lisa was claimed by another partner, Von came to their table and sat with them. As they talked Mike had a perfect opportunity to say, "If you ever need a manager for one of your plantations, I'd like to apply for the position."

"Do you really mean that, Mike? You'd give up your government job?"

"Yes, if the right opportunity came along."

"I'll certainly keep it in mind. It would be a privilege

to have someone of your training and ability to take over some of my holdings. Come see me when you're over at Nanotuma and we'll discuss this further." He turned to Thayer. "Let's finish this dance."

Instead of floating in a trance, she was acutely aware of the pressure of Von's arm, his nearness, the fragrance of his shaving lotion. The dance ended much too soon, and they returned to the table; then Von crossed the room to rejoin Lisa at the governor's table. For some reason she felt deflated, as if the spark had gone out of the evening.

It was very warm, and when Russell suggested, "Let's walk around outside," she was glad to go. He put his arm around her waist as they strolled along a path through the extensive gardens. She could smell the jasmine heavy on the night air. In the darkness, lighted faintly by the path lights, she could see the rose-flowered jatropha and jungle flame plants along the way.

"I've had a marvelous time today, Russ," she murmured. "Judy and Mike are terrific. I like them both so much. I'm so glad you invited me to come."

"I've counted the days until this weekend, and now the time has gone much too fast."

"I know."

They walked to the edge of the bay, listened to the water lap against the shore, then Russell took her in his arms and kissed her for a long time. Finally he released her and said, "I've fallen in love with you, darling."

He held her close again, kissed her eyelids, her cheek, and neck. "Will you marry me?"

118

CHAPTER 12

On the flight back to Hibiscus Lagoon, Thayer tried to sort out her tumultuous thoughts. Lisa sat next to Von and completely absorbed his attention. She ignored Thayer and relegated her to the role of being just an employee who needed transportation. No wonder Mrs. von Kuhrt felt as she did about Lisa, Thayer told herself resentfully.

Then her mind went back to Russell and his proposal. "You don't have to answer just yet," he'd said. "Perhaps I spoke too soon, but I love you, Thayer. I know that and I want you for my wife."

She'd put her arms around his neck, kissed him, and laid her head against his shoulder. "You're a wonderful, wonderful guy, Russ. Any girl would be lucky to marry you. But we hardly know each other, so give me time to think about it."

Russell was to come to Nanotuma for the weekend two weeks away. When he had driven them all to the airport, Von invited him to a celebration with a native feast and dancing in honor of the *matai*'s birthday. Russ had eagerly accepted, so Thayer knew that by then she would have to make up her mind. Was she ready to make such a lifelong commitment? She didn't know and was disturbed at the idea of hurting Russ if she had to say no.

But she was just beginning to feel settled in her niche at Seacrest and Hibiscus Lagoon. She wasn't ready for another change. She loved her home now that it was all refurbished downstairs, she was completely absorbed in

119

her job at the orchid house, and she adored her relationship with Mrs. von Kuhrt. She didn't want to give all that up and move to Pago Pago with Russell, she told herself honestly. Would he agree to a long engagement?

When they landed and drove to the house, Thayer excused herself and jumped into her car. She was anxious to leave both Von and Lisa to be by herself for a while. It had been a glorious weekend but an exhausting one. She'd made new friends with Judy and Mike and received a proposal from one of the nicest men she'd ever known. Deep in thought, she drove toward Seacrest.

The next morning, when Mrs. von Kuhrt arrived at the orchid greenhouse, she whispered, "Lisa's running true to form. I'm going to spend most of my time here or in my room."

Thayer patted her shoulder. "I'll keep you busy. Come see the worktable the carpenter made especially for you."

Thayer pushed the wheelchair into the potting room where the new worktable turned out to be exactly the right height.

"This is just perfect," Mrs. von Kuhrt exclaimed. "I can work without leaning forward, which is so tiring and painful for me."

Thayer nodded and smiled. "I'm going to have you do more pollinating this morning. You can do it on your own now."

"Yes, I'm sure I can."

"While you're doing that, I'll select plants for shipping on Thursday."

Mrs. von Kuhrt smiled. "You'd better get them there in plenty of time this time."

"I will." She smiled. "Would you like to come with me and see that I do everything right?"

120

"I'd love it. But I'm not riding in any panel truck. I'm going in my own comfortable car. In the first place I couldn't climb into the truck. So you can drive my car and I'll get one of the men around here to drive the truck and help with the unloading."

"Fine, Mrs. von Kuhrt. We'll bring your wheelchair so you can go on board to see how the freighter is loaded. Then after the plants are safely stowed on the boat, I'll take you for a ride."

Thayer soon had several orchid plants that needed pollinating in front of the older woman, then she made a selection of some of those she wanted to ship. But they needed cleaning and trimming and generally being put into salable condition.

"Now tell me all about your weekend," Mrs. von Kuhrt asked as she began her own work.

"I had one of the most wonderful times of my life." Thayer told every detail she could remember and especially raved about Judy. Finally she looked to see if the two Samoan women were within earshot, but they were spraying the plants with a fine mist in the other greenhouse.

"I'm going to tell you something in deepest confidence because I want your advice. Russell proposed to me Saturday night. I just don't know how to handle this situation."

Mrs. von Kuhrt looked up at her with a startled expression. "You hardly know each other."

"That's right. I wish he'd waited a while."

"He's a wonderful man. You shouldn't accept or reject him without a lot of careful thought."

"I agree, but I'm afraid he'll want an answer when he comes for the chief's birthday."

"Yes, Von told me he was coming." Mrs. von Kuhrt nudged pollinia out of an anther onto a piece of paper. "Isn't this something you should discuss with your

121

mother, dear? Perhaps she will come to visit you and you can put Russ off by saying you want the two of them to meet before you become engaged."

Thayer shook her head sadly. "I haven't heard from my mother for a long time." She told about their altercation. "I wish I would hear from her. She didn't even come to my graduation. You can imagine how terrible I felt." Tears swam in her eyes. "I seem to be dumping all of my troubles on you this morning."

"Does she even know that you're here in Samoa?"

"I suppose not. But she knows that Uncle Wilbur asked me to come."

Mrs. von Kuhrt patted her hand. "Dear, keep your communication lines open. Don't wait too long. Write and tell her about Wilbur's death and that you've accepted this position and you will be living here for a while. Make sure she knows your address and telephone number. Invite her and your stepfather to come for a visit at Seacrest. She may be ready for a reconciliation by this time."

Thayer considered for a long moment. "I hope so. How I hate family squabbles. I was much closer to my father than my mother but I don't want to break all my ties with her." How strange it was that she already felt more rapport with Mrs. von Kuhrt than she ever did with her own mother.

"No, you shouldn't break your ties with your family." Mrs. von Kuhrt sighed and her hand trembled as she placed the pollinia in the stigma of another plant. "I hope I don't have my own family battle. But if Von marries Lisa—" She shook her head. "It's inevitable. We'll never get along."

"I can understand."

"Well, let's not get started on Lisa. I don't want to think about her this morning. Let's go back to your problems. If you write to your mother, you can tell Russell what you've done. Say that you'd like to wait until you hear from her before you answer. Perhaps they'll have a chance to meet. That gives you a perfect excuse."

"I'm so glad I talked this over with you."

Mrs. von Kuhrt put her hand over Thayer's. "You be the one to make the first move toward patching up your quarrel with your mother. It's always easier for the injured party to apologize first."

"Apologize? Why should I apologize?" Thayer bristled and slammed her trimming shears on the bench.

"Because you presumed to pass judgment on when and if your mother should remarry! That wasn't your prerogative. That was up to your mother and the man who wanted to marry her. Actually it was none of your business."

"But my father—"

"She didn't neglect your father or cause his death, did she? She was a widow and had every legal right to marry again when she wanted to. Perhaps it was particularly convenient for that mine superintendent to marry at that time and take her back with him."

Thayer said thoughtfully, "Yes, I have to admit that it was."

"You're a sweet, dear girl and I can imagine how torn to pieces you were at the time. But you are young and have a lot to learn. You are capable of a deep, sincere love such as you had for your father. But you must realize that not everyone has that capacity for love."

"I suppose not." Somehow she'd never realized before that some people were able to love more than others.

"No doubt your mother's feelings toward your father were more superficial than yours, so she could easily transfer her affections to a new husband. You condemned her for being unfeeling and marrying too soon after your father's death, when probably she lacked the ability for real love in the first place. Remember that God would forgive her for her failings, so you'd better too."

Thayer was acutely conscious of the divine beauty of the flowers that surrounded her and of the fragrance of the moist earth in her hands. Tears swam in her eyes as she whispered, "You've given me new insight. I never—"

"My dear, why don't you forgive her and write to her?"

"I will. And I'll use that as an excuse when Russ comes weekend after next. Maybe I will want to marry him when I know him better. I'll see. But right now I want to stay in my house and work here with you. I'm not ready for another change so soon. But of course I don't want to hurt him either because he's such a terrific guy."

"Of course you don't." Mrs. von Kuhrt smiled and said, "Well, we've settled that. Let's get down to work."

That night Thayer sat at her white desk in her bedroom and tried to compose her letter. But her mind kept returning to her graduation from university when there was not one word from her mother. She recalled again the humiliation she'd felt as she made lame excuses to her friends for her mother's absence. How bleak and lonely she had felt when she had had no family present while others were surrounded by loved ones. In some ways her graduation was one of the most heartbreaking times of her life.

"I can't write! I can't," she sobbed to herself. But she remembered Mrs. von Kuhrt, that wise, wonderful woman urging her to forgive. Finally the words came, and for the first time the bitter knot of resentment she had carried in her heart for so long began to loosen.

124

She wrote about all the events that had happened since she had last seen her mother and included her address and telephone number at Seacrest so it would be possible to communicate again.

The next shipping day went much more smoothly. Mrs. von Kuhrt ordered a picnic lunch and asked for a helper to drive the truck. After the plants were safely on board the freighter before noon and all business transacted, Thayer drove Mrs. von Kuhrt's big Lincoln through the main part of town toward the winding grade up the side of the mountain.

"Isn't it ridiculous for me to have this big car when I use it so little?" the older woman asked as she patted the luxurious clipped velvet seat covering. "And it cost the earth to get it here. You can imagine! But it's comfortable and that's what I wanted."

"You deserve to have some comfort." Then Thayer laughed nervously. "I've never driven such a gorgeous car. It scares me. I hope I don't wrack it up."

"You'd better not. I don't know anyone on Nanotuma who could fix it. Think what it would cost to bring a body repairman here."

"Think what your son would do to me. That would be the last straw." Thayer laughed and then asked, "Where shall we go for our picnic? I'm starved now that I'm rid of those orchids. You don't know how relieved I feel."

"I'll show you. It's not far after you get to the summit."

Before they were up the grade, Mrs. von Kuhrt touched her arm. "Stop here a minute, dear." They looked over the edge, and she said quietly, "This is where my husband was killed. Right here. Apparently he had a heart attack and his Land-Rover went over the edge and down the mountainside. Wilbur was with him but fortunately was thrown free."

As Thayer looked down the face of the cliff horror gripped her. What a shock it must have been for Von and Mrs. von Kuhrt. Finally she murmured, "How sad for you to lose your husband so tragically."

"I've missed him very much." She was silent a moment and then said, "You can drive on now. I always like to stop a moment and pay tribute to dear Gunther when I come this way. And to dear Wilbur too. They were such close friends. Your uncle never recovered from his death. Now they are both gone."

Later Thayer stopped the car, helped Mrs. von Kuhrt into her wheelchair, and pushed her to a picnic spot near a waterfall. As they ate their lunch they listened to the cascading water and watched a nest of red-tailed tropic birds that were hidden under a wild fern. The feathers of the young were barred with black and white and the bills were dark so they blended well into the shadows. A mother bird with long, taut red and black tail feathers strutted uneasily near the nest to guard it.

"Isn't this heaven?" Mrs. von Kuhrt sighed contentedly as she nibbled on a sandwich. "You can't imagine how much I am enjoying this outing. To go on that freighter and watch them load, and now this picnic."

"I've been thinking about something and now is a good chance to ask you. The International Orchid Growers Association is having a convention and orchid show at the Royal Hawaiian Hotel in Honolulu in January. How about you and I going and exhibiting some Von Kuhrt orchids?"

The older woman stared at her in astonishment. "But I haven't gone anyplace—"

"I know you haven't. But I think we could manage fine. We could take your maid, and of course I would be right with you. I think we'd have a great time! We should start exhibiting at the big shows and build up a reputation for our plants. You should get out and meet other orchidists, and so should I."

Mrs. von Kuhrt's eyes glowed with anticipation. "I'll talk it over with Von."

"Don't say anything just yet. I promised Von I'd invite all of you for dinner while Lisa is here. I'll bring it up that evening and show him the brochures about the convention. If you approach him, he'll talk you out of it. I need to be there."

"That's right. You're the only one who can stand up to him in an argument. And we'd love to come to dinner. That'll help get through one evening with Lisa. When do you want us?"

"Better come Saturday evening, then I can help Fetu get ready."

"We'll be there. But it won't be near as much fun as when Von, Tupuasa, and I all dropped in on you unexpectedly. We had such a good time that evening. Lisa wasn't there to spoil everything. Fortunately Von asked her to go with him today so I didn't have to invite her along."

"I doubt if she'd come. I think watching them load the freighter and picnicking with us would leave her cold."

"She practices the piano all the time. I must admire her for being so devoted to her music. Come over early next week for dinner and hear her play."

On Saturday Thayer made careful preparations for her dinner party. She displayed her green and gold orchid plants to advantage and suspended the hanging baskets of ferns from the ceiling. While Fetu roasted a suckling pig and prepared breadfruit and coconut, Thayer polished the silver, pressed the linen, and set the table. Toward evening she stopped long enough to shower and put on her yellow jersey dress. Finally she was ready and braced herself for a session with Lisa.

But with Von present, Lisa went out of her way to be charming. She complimented Thayer on the appearance of the house and had much to say to Fetu when the food was served. But as she spoke to Von about their mutual friends in Western Samoa, she managed to exclude Thayer and Mrs. von Kuhrt. Later as they played bridge, she was Von's partner and he kept his attention focused on her.

At the end of the evening Thayer brought out the brochures about the orchid convention in January. "I think we should exhibit and become better known among the other growers. By that time your mother will have some background and experience in orchid culture."

Von turned to his mother. "Do you think you could manage?"

"Yes, with my maid and Thayer I could. Of course I'll get tired and perhaps have some pain but I do right at home. I would enjoy it enormously."

"May I send in our reservations, then?" Thayer asked. "We could always cancel later if necessary."

Von nodded. "Get a check from the accountant."

Before she left, Mrs. von Kuhrt had a chance to whisper, "I can't believe my ears. Von made no objection at all."

Thayer squeezed the older woman's hand.

Mrs. von Kuhrt went on, "Everything was so lovely, dear. Thank you for asking us. It gave me a break. Come to dinner Tuesday night and that will take care of another evening."

Thayer nodded. "Perhaps Lisa will play for us." She gave the older woman a hug. "I'll see you Monday. Just spend all the time you can with the orchids."

After dinner Tuesday evening, they sat in the living room with Lisa at the piano. How beautiful she looked with her flowered chiffon dinner dress falling in soft folds around her. "I'll begin with a Chopin's nocturne and then play Debussy's *Suite Bergamasque*," she announced and then began to play with skill fit for the concert stage. Von sat with his eyes on her, transfixed with admiration. When she had finished, they clapped enthusiastically.

"Now I'll play one of my favorites, Mendelssohn's Scherzo in E minor, Opus Sixteen. Number Two. This scherzo, which has a transfigured staccato étude has a dynamic profile ranging from pianissimo to fortissimo." Lisa spoke only to Von as if the other two women were so untrained in music that they couldn't understand her.

When the last note was struck, Von clapped vigorously and leaped to his feet. "Bravo! Bravo! What a treat! You should be on the concert stage."

"Well, I am giving some concerts this fall. I'm also going on tour again with the symphony."

"You play superbly, Lisa," Thayer said, but the pianist glanced her way without acknowledging the compliment, as if her opinion was of little worth. Thayer sank back into her chair, feeling inadequate and thoroughly put down.

Thayer watched the expression on Von's face while he leaned over the keyboard, looking through the music to choose the next selection. It was as if the beautiful pianist had cast a spell over him, as if he couldn't get enough of her music and her beauty.

Thayer's eyes darted back and forth between the two at the piano as she sat trembling inside with misery, wishing she were home. Lisa was too formidable with her talent and it was agony watching Von look at her with such adoration. Mrs. von Kuhrt was right; inevitably the engagement would be announced soon. Perhaps at the chief's birthday celebration. She tried to dismiss all thoughts of Von and Lisa.

* * *

The next morning, when Thayer was busy moving delicate Philippine moth orchids into a shadier part of the greenhouse, she looked up to see Lisa, instead of a maid, pushing Mrs. von Kuhrt along the walkway. "What's going on here?" she asked herself aloud. There was some ulterior motive, of that Thayer was positive. Unconsciously she put up her guard as she went to greet the two women.

"Good morning," she called. "Come right in."

Lisa looked especially slender and attractive in her pale blue pants and sleeveless top. "I just had to see what you were doing around here. Aren't these orchids breathtaking?" She gazed around at the display.

"I never tire of looking at them," Mrs. von Kuhrt answered enthusiastically, but her face was especially gray and strained this morning. Was she in extreme pain or had she realized, like Thayer herself, how emotionally involved Von was with Lisa and it was getting to her? "The more I learn about orchids the more fascinated I become."

She maneuvered her wheelchair until she was under the worktable, but as she reached for one of the plants that Thayer had placed there, she winced with pain.

Lisa ran forward and moved the orchid closer. She looked up at Thayer. "Really Von and I are so concerned about this project of Mother von Kuhrt's. We don't think she is up to working so much."

"Isn't that for Mrs. von Kuhrt to decide?" Thayer asked.

"Of course it is!" the older woman snapped. "I can assure you I suffered a great deal of pain long before we had orchids here. And I'm much better since I've been able to do this."

"But, Mother von Kuhrt, I know of the most wonderful rest home in Auckland." Lisa's smooth voice was

130

most persuasive. "You have friends there who would come to see you. You could get proper medical treatment too. You should be in therapy."

"Therapy!" Thayer cried. "Isn't this therapy to be here among these orchids? To do work she's genuinely interested in?"

"I've been in therapy for ten years," Mrs. von Kuhrt said as she carefully studied the reproductive parts of the orchid plant in front of her. "I have the finest Jacuzzi and all the exercise equipment available right in my own house."

Thayer determined to change the subject. "Now that you're here, Lisa, let me show you around. Von has such a well-planned operation here." She eased the other girl toward the collector's items.

As graciously as possible Thayer took Lisa on a tour of both greenhouses and the potting room. She gradually headed her toward the front entrance, hoping her difficult visitor would leave.

When they were in the doorway and out of hearing range of the others, Lisa turned on Thayer angrily. "Von and I mean it! You shouldn't encourage Mrs. von Kuhrt to spend so much time here. It's not good for her. She's been failing terribly of late."

Thayer pulled herself to her full height. "Since Mrs. von Kuhrt owns half of this plantation and a great deal of this orchid department, don't you think she has the right to come here if she wants to? And I, for one, love having her!"

"You're just an employee, Thayer. You've taken too much authority on yourself. You're forgetting your place!"

Thayer refused to be intimidated. "You're forgetting that I'm a well-trained floriculturist holding down a responsible position here with authority. Also that my uncle was a planter and the Von Kuhrts' closest friend, so you don't need to pull that 'just an employee' line on me."

"Your idea of taking Mother von Kuhrt to the orchid convention is ridiculous. She's not up to such an undertaking."

"On what do you base that conclusion? Are you a doctor as well as a pianist?" she demanded, undaunted.

"Well, anyway, I've highly recommended that Mrs. von Kuhrt go in a rest home for proper care and treatment. Von agrees with me. We'll thank you to keep your opinions to yourself after this! We'll decide what's best for her welfare."

An angry flush darkened Thayer's face and her voice rose. "Her welfare? Come off of it! You're not concerned about *her* welfare! And you're not fooling me a bit! You just want to get rid of her so she won't be around here when you're mistress of Hibiscus Lagoon!"

"How dare you, you snip! And mind your own business." She turned and hurried toward the house.

As Thayer moved away from the doorway she caught a glimpse of a khaki-clad figure in the building next door. She knew that it was Von, and she had an uncomfortable feeling that he had overheard them.

CHAPTER 13

The cool evening breeze off the bay billowed the new panel curtains in the study as Thayer sat at her uncle's desk and sorted through his papers. She discarded old letters, newspaper clippings, and personal bills but she put to one side any papers that related to the management of the plantation.

The next day Russell would arrive on the interisland launch, and she looked forward to seeing him. Perhaps she was on the verge of falling in love with him. Anyway a delightful weekend was in store with dinner at Hibiscus Lagoon the next evening and the chief's birthday celebration all afternoon and evening on Saturday. Even the prospect of spending some time with Lisa didn't dampen her anticipation.

It was obvious that Lisa just wanted to get rid of Mrs. von Kuhrt by shunting her off to a rest home in Auckland. Surely Von would not let her get by with that. Anyway Lisa had stayed away from the orchid house so Mrs. von Kuhrt had had a few hours of contentment each day.

Thayer found a worn address book back in one of the desk drawers. She riffled through it, started to throw the book away, and then put it back in its place. She might need it eventually, she told herself.

When the telephone rang, Thayer expected to hear Russell's voice, but it was a woman's.

"Thayer, dear, this is Mother."

"Mother! What a surprise!" A wave of thankfulness

washed over her. "How wonderful to hear your voice! How are you?"

"I'm fine," she said tentatively and rushed on. "I was so glad to receive your letter. I can't tell you how happy it made me feel. I'm so sorry we had a misunderstanding."

"I'm sorry too, Mom, so let's put it behind us. . . . As I said in my letter, it was really none of my business when you got married again."

"We both said some harsh things but, yes, let's forget them now and start fresh. It's too bad about Wilbur's death, but I'm glad you can live in his home and that you have a job."

"I love my work, Mom. It's exactly what I was trained to do." It was amazing how clearly she could hear her mother; it was as if she were speaking from next door instead of miles away. "How's Tom?"

"Well, he's fine and he insisted that I telephone you instead of writing. He sends his love and thanks you for your invitation to come to Samoa. In fact he gets his vacation in October and if it's convenient for you we'd like to come then."

"Mother, how marvelous!"

"We can stop in Hawaii and Fiji as well as Samoa. We might go on to New Zealand too."

"It sounds like a perfect trip! And I'll be so glad to see you." She fought for control. "I've missed you, Mom."

Her mother's voice shook. "And I've missed you. Nothing could have meant more to me than that letter. You'll never know. I'll be delighted to see you again. It's been a long time. I'll hang up now, dear, but I'll write soon and we'll see you in October."

"Good-bye, Mom. Thanks for the call." Her chin quivered, and when she replaced the receiver, she put her head in her arms and sobbed with relief. She had been torn to pieces over her father's death and her break with her mother. At last the wound could heal.

She could hardly wait to tell Mrs. von Kuhrt about this call. How grateful she was to Von's mother for urging her to write to her mother. Now she and her mother could exchange letters and telephone calls and have a normal relationship again. What a wonderful, wonderful relief! She realized how much she had suffered because of the rift. Apparently her mother had grieved too.

On Friday afternoon she saw Russell briefly and later he called for her in Von's car to take her to Hibiscus Lagoon for dinner. On the way he pulled off the road, stopped under a banyan tree, and took her in his arms.

"Oh, darling, I've been counting the hours." He kissed her tenderly and then asked, "What about us? I have to know."

"Russ, you're the dearest person I ever knew. But I want to be absolutely fair with you and be sure that we should get married. My mother and stepfather are coming to see me early in October. I want you to meet them and for them to meet you before we become engaged. Would you be willing to wait for an answer until then?"

He thought a minute, then kissed the tips of her fingers. "I guess so. That's only two and a half months away. I'll admit I'm disappointed; I'd hoped for an answer tonight. But perhaps we should know one another better." He held her to him and she felt his hand slide over her breast, around her waist and press against her thin jersey dress at her back. "It's just that I want you so much."

As he kissed her again, her heart thudded painfully, her cheeks burned, and a small gnawing hunger for him flamed through her. Of course she was falling in love with him. It would be so easy to say yes and be married

135

when her parents came. But she held back. She wasn't quite ready.

"It's just that I want to be wholehearted, Russ. You deserve more than half-measures. I think I've been through so many changes this past year, I'm still sort of numb. All I seem to want for a while is to crawl in my niche and stay there."

"I do understand, darling. And you have been through a lot of adjustments—your father's death, leaving your college, selling your family home, leaving all those lifelong friends, and then coming here to find your uncle dead. I'll be patient until you are ready."

Finally she pulled away from him and said in a shaky voice, "We'd better go on. The Von Kuhrts are expecting us." She laughed and reached for a tissue. "You have lipstick on your mouth. Here, I'll wipe it off."

He patted her hair in place. "You're so pretty, Thayer. I love looking at you."

Soon they arrived at Hibiscus Lagoon, and with two handsome men to charm, Lisa was in her element. If she felt any resentment toward Thayer, she didn't show it.

As they sat on the terrace before dinner Thayer sipped her drink and looked at the other girl in her flame-colored chiffon dress. There was no question that Lisa had impeccable taste and knew how to dress and groom herself to make the most of her incredible beauty.

While Lisa monopolized the men, Thayer turned to Mrs. von Kuhrt, who looked haggard. Having Lisa around so much was taking its toll on the older woman, and Thayer's heart ached for her. As she talked about her parents' impending visit she wondered what Mrs. von Kuhrt would do when Von and Lisa were married. It was unthinkable that she would have to leave this

136

lovely home that was hers, where she'd lived for so long and raised her son.

The next day, the festivities for the chief or *matai*'s birthday began in midafternoon with a fish drive. While a large crowd watched from the shore, nets were set in a V shape in the bay. Then men and boys waded out into the water, carrying woven palm swatters. They began to swat the top of the water to set up vibrations to disturb and confuse the fish. As the men walked toward the center of the net the tempo of the swatting quickened. In panic the fish swam away from the source of the noise right into the nets.

Then the men raised the dripping nets filled with wiggling fish. They picked out the ones they wanted for the upcoming feast and immediate use, then threw the rest back in the water. It was a humane, centuries-old method of fishing.

After the fish drive Thayer and Russell followed a group of children through the palm trees to a waterfall that cascaded over lava rock to form a large pool at the foot before it became a stream that flowed into the bay. The children lined up at the top of the falls and took turns sliding down the smooth boulders.

"If we only had our bathing suits, we could do that too," Thayer said regretfully.

"Actually we could do it if you want to," he said mischievously. "We'd soon dry."

"I'd better not. I'm afraid I'd be a mess and have to go home to change before the feast."

Russell took her hand. "That's true. And you look very lovely."

When the children tired of sliding down the waterfall, one of the older boys climbed a tree by the side of the pool and sat on a branch until it bent toward the water. A piece of rope dangled from a branch, so Russell jumped up to grab hold of it. One by one the children climbed up the tree and sat on the branch while he jounced them up and down until they tumbled off into the pool below.

As she watched and listened to the children squeal with delight she thought that far too many people trudged through life without any real fun. But the Samoans enjoyed themselves, the company of their friends, and the beauty of their environment to the full.

She watched Russell and thought fondly, *He's about the greatest. The kids adore him. They have an instinct for kind, good people.* Then why did she hesitate? Why wait? She should tell Russ at once that she'd marry him. She'd never find a finer man.

When Russell rejoined her, she said aloud, "What a good time the kids have here in Samoa!"

"They sure do. They share everything with each other so that they grow up unselfish; everything is for the community rather than the individual. I hope we'll always live here and raise a family." Russell squeezed her hand. "I like kids, don't you?"

Thayer nodded. "They seem to like you too." He would make a wonderful father.

Finally Thayer and Russell walked back to the beach to where Chief Malietoa, head of the Upo family, held court. They joined the others who sat in a circle in the shade of the palm trees around the old man who was so joyfully celebrating his seventy-fifth birthday.

For the benefit of his *papalagi* guests, the *matai* spoke in English, but he pointed to his own people. "Samoa is the very heart of Polynesia. Be proud of your heritage."

The chief went on, "This is God's country too. You *papalagi* never took Christianity seriously. We do. You talk about Christianity but we live it."

138

Von nodded. "I think you're right."

"I know I'm right. Remember when Pope Paul the Sixth came to Polynesia in nineteen seventy? He celebrated Mass in Samoa, not in New Zealand or other bigger countries. He chose our country because we're the land of Christian light. He said so."

Russell nodded. "Everyone agrees that you're the true Christians. I hear that everyplace I go."

The chief looked around proudly. "Did all of you hear my good friend? Everyone knows about us."

Then the chief rose and led the men to the meeting-house for the kava ceremony. But Thayer and Lisa stayed with the women to watch the final preparations for the feast.

An enormous pig had been roasting in a pit all day. But another pit or *umu* had been dug for the rest of the food. Some of the women piled rocks on an open fire in the pit. When the rocks were hot and the fire burned out, women put leaf-wrapped fish, chicken, bananas, lobsters, and taro in the pit on top of the rocks. More leaves and finally sacks were placed over the roasting food.

Of course women had been arriving all afternoon with salads and cakes, which were taken to one of the *fales* in the village.

After the kava ceremony and while the food continued to cook, they watched young men throw spears at a coconut shell nailed to the top of the pole. Finally gifts were presented to the chief. Thayer brought him the finest of her ceremonial mats, and she could see that in due time she would have them all returned to these good people. There was little sense of personal possession among them, as everything belonged to the community.

Before the feast was over, it had grown dark, so it

was time for the torches to be lighted. First two handsome young men blew on enormous conch shells and then two others ran around lighting the torches from the ones flaming in their hands.

Finally it was time for dancing. First a young man performed an ancient knife dance with each end lighted with dancing flames. Then with great skill and authenticity, Tahitian, hula, and war dances were performed.

Thayer sat contentedly near Russell with her back against a tree. Since he'd been willing to wait for her answer to his proposal, there was no stress to worry her. But she was already feeling possessive toward him so she put her hand on his shoulder. They'd go along as they were for a while but she felt sure that she would marry him sooner or later. Kind, generous, well-educated, and attractive, he was outgoing and well liked. He'd be a good family man, as well. What more did she want?

Not far away, in the light of a flickering torch, Thayer could see Lisa leaning against Von's shoulder. She smiled to herself as she remembered her welcoming kava ceremony and later when Von had translated the words of the talking chief. "The gods sent you here because I needed a wife. Someone young, beautiful, and charming who would make a good mistress at Hibiscus Lagoon and bear many children for me."

Thayer watched Von pull Lisa to him and kiss her on the mouth. A stab of searing jealousy cut into her. Shocked, she sat up and stared into the darkness. She was jealous of Lisa, terribly, bitterly jealous of her; it seemed to permeate her bloodstream to every cell.

Then Thayer knew the truth. She could never marry Russell. Without realizing or admitting it, she was in love with Von.

140

CHAPTER 14

She leaned back against the tree trunk almost in a state of shock. How could she fall in love with a man who had robbed her uncle? Who had literally taken her inheritance from her? And she had the proof in a folder back at her house.

She looked at him again. The nearby flickering torch illuminated his handsome, aristocratic face. She was aware of his height, his strength, his dynamic, forceful personality. She loved him with all her heart and for the first time she realized the truth. She'd always felt this violent reaction to his presence. A certain sensual crosscurrent passed between them like an electrical charge. But how could she love a man who kept her in this constant state of turmoil? She was never relaxed around him; she was always on her mettle.

As the light and shadows played across his body, she studied the shape of his head, the strong, beautiful planes of his face, his bone structure, his becoming hair and mustache. There was something about the set of his shoulders, the way he stood and swung his arms, the way he walked that commanded respect and obedience. He exuded power and leadership and exciting virility. And she loved him.

She listened to the throbbing drums that the Samoans were beating in the darkness. Tears gathered in her eyes and rolled down her cheeks. She turned away and wiped them off with the back of her hand. A girl was dancing the pagan, primitive *siva-siva* dance with her torso gyrating to a crescendo of passion that must have shocked the early missionaries. As Russell watched the dancer with rapt attention he didn't notice Thayer's distress.

It was awful to contemplate the realization of her love. Von had his arm around Lisa; he looked as if he wanted to kiss her again. Thayer felt a stab of pain as she thought of them together as man and wife.

Nothing but heartbreak lay ahead. She knew that she couldn't accept Russell's proposal in view of her feelings toward Von. He would be crushed, of course, but he deserved a wife that would be completely devoted to him and not someone whose heart was elsewhere. She put her hand on the sand beneath her and felt the grains bite into her skin. The drums beat on and on in a wild frenzy adding to her own turbulence.

Finally the evening was over so she rose to her feet and turned shakily to Russell. "Do you mind taking me home now, Russ? I feel ill. I'm afraid something I ate upset me terribly."

"You don't look well. Darling, you're white as a sheet! I'll speak to Von and we'll cut right out of here."

She slumped in a miserable huddle in the car. Heartsick, she just wanted to get home and be by herself, away from everyone—Russ and Von included.

The next morning Russell telephoned and she begged off seeing him, saying that she'd better stay in bed. He answered that he understood and would devote the day to visiting plantations. She put on a caftan, and sat down at her uncle's desk. Not only had Von cheated her out of her legacy from her uncle but now she couldn't find happiness in marriage with Russell or anyone else. Anger boiled in her. Damn him! She wanted to strike at Von and hurt him. She couldn't bear the thought of staying on at Hibiscus Lagoon after he married.

She slammed the folder on the desk and paced the

floor restlessly. She had to do something: She was too uptight to read or sew. Finally she opened the door to the closet in the study and decided to go through the material stored there.

Regardless of what she decided to do eventually, she had to dispose of her uncle's personal things before she left Seacrest. It wasn't fair to him to leave everything for strangers to inspect. Of course he had expected to return when he left, so he wouldn't have everything in order. A good place to begin was right in this closet.

First she tugged at some heavy boxes on the closet floor and found that they were cases of rum, gin, and bourbon. Apparently Russell's story about Wilbur's heavy drinking was all too true.

In one corner of the closet she found a tall canvas case. She pulled it out, unzipped the cover, and revealed a tripod with an attached telescope and a spirit level mounted on a vertical axis. She recognized them as surveying instruments. Then she noticed an engraved metal plate on the tripod with the name EDWARD CRANE. She'd seen that name before on some of the old letters she'd thrown away. Apparently he was another planter but he lived in Western Samoa instead of American Samoa. From the correspondence she had seen, she surmised that he had been a close friend of Wilbur's.

No doubt her uncle had borrowed the instruments so the first step would be to write this Edward Crane and find out if he wanted the instruments returned and how best to send them. She rummaged through the desk and found the worn address book with its listing for Crane. She immediately sat down and wrote her letter so it could go off the next day.

She spent several hours going through the material in the closet and set aside boxes to discuss with Fetu before discarding them. As she worked her mind went back to her situation. Should she tell Russell at once that she could never marry him? No, she could wait awhile; they'd already agreed to that.

Should she stay on with her job at Hibiscus Lagoon? Actually now she could leave anytime. She had contact with her mother again so she could always borrow the airfare and enough money to tide her over until she got a new job. So far it had taken her salary to pay her bill for the curtains, upholstery material, and paint.

Where could she go? She didn't want to join her mother in a remote mining town. She had friends in Minnesota of course, but how could she get a job as a floriculturist since it was not a major flower-producing state?

She loved the beauty of Samoa and the kind, gentle people. She loved Mrs. von Kuhrt and the fascinating hours they spent together working with the plants. Soon they would be ready to hybridize and perhaps create new varieties of orchids to sell. It was an exciting, wonderful project. She looked around her house. She loved it too. She didn't want to leave Samoa at all. But how could she stay? It would be kind of hell, a self-imposed torture to see Von and Lisa together day after day.

Finally she finished the closet so she went into the living room and stretched out on the sofa and fell asleep. It was late in the afternoon when the doorbell rang and she awakened. When she went to the door, Von and Russell stood there.

Von said, "We're on our way home so we dropped by to see how you were."

"Feeling better, Thayer?" Russell asked.

"Yes, thanks, I think I am. Come on in." She led the way into the living room, painfully conscious of her bare feet, her rumpled hair, and the absence of makeup on her face. She sat on the davenport.

144

The men sat down and looked at her. Since she had no prospects of marrying either of them, it didn't matter how raunchy she looked, she decided.

"Did you suffer from food poisoning, do you think?" Von asked. "Russ and I are okay."

"No, not really. But I think it was some spice that didn't agree with me. I guess I'm not quite a Polynesian yet. It all takes some getting used to."

"That's true." Von waved his arm around. "Didn't Thayer do a great job fixing up this place? You remember what it was like when Wilbur was here."

"I sure do." Russ leaned back in his chair and touched the cushions. "It was all going to seed, like poor old Wilbur. But he was out of it so much of the time, I guess it didn't matter."

Von grinned. "Better cool it. Thayer fights like a tiger if you badmouth Wilbur." He looked around. "As I've said before, Thayer, I had no idea you were such a nest-builder. This looks great."

Russell leaned forward. "Of course I'm hoping she'll build a nest for me someday. I've asked her to marry me."

Annoyance flared up in Thayer as she tucked her feet under her caftan. "Really, Russ, I don't think that's anyone's business but ours." Why did he make such a remark? Now he would be more embarrassed than ever when she refused him.

Von's face narrowed and a strange expression passed over his face. Thayer couldn't read it, but he looked almost stricken. Finally he said, "Are congratulations in order?"

Russell answered, "No, not yet. We're waiting until her parents come in October. I hope they'll approve of me, and then we'll see."

After a silence Von changed the subject. "Before we

145

leave Seacrest, I want you to look at the new banana suckers."

She studied the men as they talked about raising bananas. They were so different, a person couldn't compare them. But they were two of the most attractive men she'd ever known. How amazing to find them both way off here in a tiny island in the vast Pacific. She leaned her head against the back of the sofa. She couldn't marry Russell; it was Von who had the magic for her. Her heart twisted painfully. Would she ever get over her feeling for him?

Finally Von said, "Do you feel up to coming over for dinner with us tonight? Of course you're more than welcome."

"Thanks, but I'll just have a little soup and go back to bed. I want to be able to work tomorrow." She couldn't subject herself to another evening of being with Lisa, Von, and Russ and of trying to hide her pain and hopelessness.

"Don't try to come if you don't feel up to it, Thayer. Your work will wait for you."

Thayer smiled. "Not this week. We're shipping Thursday, you know. But I'll be all right if I get a good night's rest and don't eat anything."

Von stood up then. "Come on, Russ, I want your advice about something."

She walked to the door with them. "I'll see you both in the morning." She braced herself against the doorframe as if she were waiting for a blow.

Russell leaned toward her and kissed her on the mouth. "Take care, darling."

Von mocked him and copied, "Take care, darling," and kissed her too, but under his teasing expression there was a tenseness about his face.

A twist of pain wrenched through her. She slammed the door and leaned against it while tears sprang in her

146

eyes. Would it always be like this? Longing for a man, knowing all the while he would never be hers. Finally she ran up the stairs, threw herself on her bed, and cried.

She was relieved the next day when Von took Russell to the interisland launch. She wanted no intimate conversations with Russ yet, as she had to think what she was going to say to him. She didn't want to encourage him and have him build even more false hopes.

Even Mrs. von Kuhrt became absorbed in her work and had little to say, so Thayer went about her work, grateful for her orderly routine in the midst of the upheaval in her life.

That night after dinner Thayer sat at her uncle's desk and again looked through the folder marked EVIDENCE. There were the exact dates when Von took certain equipment away. Sprayers and huge harvesting rigs that meant an investment of thousands of dollars. Tractors and trucks were listed with their license numbers. The evidence was indisputable.

Filled with disgust and self-loathing, she asked herself why she fell in love with him when she knew very well what he was like under that handsome exterior. It seemed incredible that she had so little control over her emotions.

She spread the papers out on the desk and studied them. Surely there'd be some attorney who would represent her in court. Don Alo was mesmerized by the Von Kuhrt name, but not all lawyers in Samoa would be so gullible. No doubt he had pulled other illegal deals so he had enemies who would testify in her behalf.

She heard dogs barking outside and Fetu go to the door, but she paid little attention. She was deeply engrossed in reading one of the income tax returns when

Fetu spoke from the doorway, "Miss Elwood, Mr. von Kuhrt is here. He would like to see you."

Thayer looked up. Fetu had gone, but Von came into the room. "Hi." She waved him toward a chair. "This is an unexpected visit."

"Well, something has just come up," Von began as he sat down. "Lisa's mother telephoned a little while ago that Mr. Campbell has had a severe heart attack. He's just been rushed to the hospital in Apia. It looks very serious. I'm going to fly Lisa there early in the morning."

"Oh, I'm so sorry."

"There's something very important that I would like you to do for me. When you take the shipment of orchid plants to the freighter on Thursday, I want you to see if some special equipment I've ordered has come. It should be on that boat." He waved an invoice. "It has to be handled with the greatest care because it's very expensive and delicate."

"I'll see if it's on the freighter."

"If it is, you're to get some men to load it carefully for you in the panel truck. Pick the men that you know are the most reliable. Then you yourself are to bring it to Hibiscus Lagoon for me."

"Then what shall I do with it?"

"Leave it in the truck until you get hold of Vaoifi. As you know, he is the one responsible for all the equipment. No one else is to touch it. It's to be in his charge until I get back. I know I can trust you to take care of this matter."

"I will, of course. Please tell Lisa how sorry I am about her father."

Von stood up, stepped near her. He tossed the invoice onto the desk behind her, then he just looked at her. Finally he murmured, "Thayer, there's something between us." His voice was very close; her breath was coming fast. "My God, I don't know what it is!" She sensed it rather than saw when his arms reached out for her and she was drawn firmly and deftly close.

She could feel the warmth of his body. Her lips parted to protest, but there were no clear or coherent thoughts in her head to utter, and then his mouth was pressed bruisingly against hers. It happened completely without her consent and for a long moment she lost every shred of self-control. Her whole body was filled with a longing, a fever, and she felt wave after wave of a sensation that was half pain and half ecstasy.

Finally she came to her senses. He didn't love her. He was going to marry Lisa. No doubt he kissed that woman like this all the time. But she would be his wife; perhaps they now were even engaged. She struggled against him and pushed him away.

"Leave me alone!" Her anger boiled. "I despise you, Eiland von Kuhrt!"

He looked as if he'd been whiplashed. At first all the color drained from his face as if he were in shock, and then it darkened with fury. He stepped away from her. "Don't worry, I'll never touch you again!"

Her control snapped. All the rage and resentment she had felt against him for taking advantage of Uncle Wilbur, for getting control of Seacrest, for ruining her inheritance, surged and rocketed through her. "See that you don't, you rotten thief! You stole everything from Uncle Wilbur. Now it's all yours!"

"What are you saying?" There was something frightening about his anger. A savage maleness that was menacing. It could turn into rage. A violence.

Her own wrath matched his. "I'm saying that you're a thief! I've got the proof right here." She turned and thumped on the papers on top of the desk. "I'm going to bring you to justice, Von, if it's the last thing I ever do!"

CHAPTER 15

How thankful Thayer felt when she reported to work the next day, knowing that Von was gone. The look on his face before he'd stormed out of her house made her blood turn to ice. He had been enraged. How foolish of her to threaten him; she must have been out of her mind, she told herself. If she could only take back the words that had spurted out. He'd be a dangerous adversary, and besides, she had tipped her hand. He would have all the time in the world to work out a defense. Well, he was gone now and she wouldn't have to face him for several days.

She felt tangled in web of mixed emotions—anger, love, passion, resentment, hate, and most of all regret. She wished that her outburst had never taken place. If Von had only left right after he had given her the instructions about the equipment, she wouldn't be in this awkward position.

Thayer could hardly wait for Mrs. von Kuhrt to come so she wouldn't think about the disastrous scene with Von. When his mother arrived in midmorning, she looked like a different person. Relaxed, rested, and exultant. After they were alone, she exclaimed, "How wonderful to have Lisa gone. What a relief! I've ordered a special lunch for us and you're to come to help me celebrate."

"I'll do that. But I am sorry about her father."

"I am too, of course. I know him and he's a fine man even if he has spoiled his daughter rotten. Spare me from Lisa!" She manuevered herself into position under her worktable. "If she marries Von, she'll try to shunt me off to a rest home. You wait and see. She won't keep me here."

"Surely Von wouldn't agree to that!" Thayer brought some Cattleya orchids to the older woman. "After all, you're one of the owners here. You must have some rights."

"Of course I do. But Lisa'll win, no matter what. It'll kill me to leave and go into a rest home, but I swear I won't last long when she's here running the place."

Thayer gave her a little hug and smiled. "Nothing will happen for a while so we can just relax for now."

Mrs. von Kuhrt put her hand on Thayer's arm and looked up at her. "If only you and Von. . . . I've hoped and prayed that it would work out for you two." She sighed. "You're the daughter I've never had and always longed for. But now it's you and Russell and Von and Lisa."

If Mrs. von Kuhrt knew the true situation, how surprised she would be, Thayer thought. She said comfortingly, "I'm not going to marry anyone for a long, long time. I'm going to stay at Seacrest and work here as long as I can. And I'm going to keep your nose to the grindstone too."

But Mrs. von Kuhrt wasn't quite ready to let go of her pet subject. "All the Samoans believe that the talking chief's prophecy will come true. That you'll be the next mistress of Hibiscus Lagoon."

"How can they think that when they saw Lisa with Von at the chief's birthday feast? And Russell and I together?"

"As far as they are concerned, the gods sent you here to be Von's wife. None of them likes Lisa, but you've won their hearts completely. You're the one they want."

Thayer shrugged but regret tugged at her heart. "I'm sure Von will choose his own wife—when and if he

151

wants one. Neither the talking chief nor anyone else will have anything to say about it. Besides, I'm sure I drive him up the wall."

"I wouldn't say that, dear. Sometimes the way he talks about you, I get my hopes all up."

"Don't get any false hopes, Mrs von Kuhrt. Now I must get down to work. There's a shipping day this week, you know."

As she chose the plants for shipping and put them aside for her helpers to trim and pack, she thought about Von. If only the awful confrontation between them had never taken place. If only he loved her instead of Lisa. If only he'd never gained control of Seacrest by underhanded means. If! If! If!

After their scene last night, he'd despise her rather than just be semifriendly as he was before. Also by helping Lisa through this present crisis, he'd be drawn even closer to her. It was just a matter of time before Von and Lisa would announce their wedding plans.

Work was her salvation. Work so hard that there was no time to think too much, she told herself, and that you could drop off to sleep with exhaustion when you went to bed. She put long hours in at the orchid house, got a fine shipment of plants ready and spent her evenings sorting through the things in her uncle's bedroom. At least things would be shipshape when she had to leave.

On Thursday she met the freighter with her plant shipment and found that the special equipment for Von was indeed on board. She chose the most reliable men at the dock to place the huge, heavy box in the panel truck and then brought it safely to Hibiscus Lagoon to put it in Vaoifi's care. Von could never say that she didn't carry out his orders to the letter.

Von was always under the surface of her thoughts. No matter how absorbed she'd become in some work, an image of him, so tall, so masculine, and so heart-breakingly attractive, would project itself on her mind to aggravate the sorrow she felt. Why did she ever fall in love with him? It was all so futile. Nothing but heartache and frustration lay ahead for her. The break was complete between them; they couldn't even be friends from now on.

Thursday evening she cleaned out her uncle's dresser drawers. She placed his shirts, underwear, and socks in boxes for Fetu to distribute among her needy friends. She was still working when the extension telephone by Wilbur's bed jangled. When she answered, a strange voice with a strong New Zealand accent said, "Miss Elwood, this is Edward Crane."

"Oh, yes. The man with the surveying instruments. I'm glad to hear from you."

"Well, I would like to have my instruments back. I'd loaned them to Wilbur sometime ago."

"Shall I ship them?"

"No, I ran into Von here in Apia and told him about them. He's flying home for the weekend and bringing me with him. I'd like to have a visit with Mrs. von Kuhrt. I'll just pick up my things and bring them back with me, if you don't mind."

"That will be fine."

"Will you call Hibiscus Lagoon and tell Mrs. von Kuhrt that Von and I will be there sometime tomorrow afternoon?"

"Yes, of course. How is Mr. Campbell, do you know?"

"Somewhat better, I believe. At least Von feels he can leave for the weekend."

When she called Hibiscus Lagoon, Mrs. von Kuhrt invited her to dinner on Saturday night but Thayer declined. It would be too painful to face Von, so she said, "Mr. Crane wants to visit with you. He said so. If I'm there he won't feel free to reminisce about all your old friends that I don't know. I'll take a rain check this time."

"All right, if you insist, dear. I'll send him over for his instruments on Saturday morning, though. Then, if something unexpected comes up with Lisa's father, they'll be ready to leave at once."

Much to her relief Thayer did not see Von on Friday. Perhaps he would return to Apia before she had to confront him.

But Saturday morning Edward Crane, a middle-aged, sandy-haired man, drove into her driveway in one of the older station wagons from Hibiscus Lagoon. He was a straightforward, likable man. When he shook hands at the front door, he said sadly, "Doesn't seem right that Wilbur's not here. I can't get used to the idea. I spent many a holiday here with him."

"It was a shock for all of us. I came from Minnesota to live with him but never had the chance. But do come in, Mr. Crane."

When they walked through the living room, Mr. Crane whistled. "Say now, it never looked like this in all the years I've visited here. Many a time I offered to help slap some paint on these walls but couldn't get Wilbur started."

"It was quite an undertaking for all of us here," Thayer said and smiled. "I don't blame him for putting it off."

They entered the study and sat down. The surveying instruments leaned against the closet door. When Mr. Crane saw them, he nodded, "I'll be glad to get them back. I use them on my plantation sometimes."

"You were quite a good friend of Wilbur's, weren't you?" Thayer reached for the coffee percolator and poured them each a cup.

"Yes, just about the best. My wife died about ten

154

years ago and I got in the habit of coming here whenever it got too lonesome for me. Of course Wilbur was awfully close to Gunther von Kuhrt until he was gone."

They chatted awhile about the funeral. "I was there, but you wouldn't remember." Edward Crane settled back in his chair with his coffee cup. "Guess we were all a bunch of strangers to you. It's a shame Wilbur couldn't have lived to enjoy your company, miss. He never had a family around before."

Thayer finished her coffee, thought a minute, and then made up her mind. She needed advice desperately, and perhaps this New Zealand planter who knew her uncle so well was just the one to give it to her.

"Mr. Crane, something puzzles me very much and I'd like to talk to someone about it. I need advice and I don't know anyone else who could help me." She opened the desk drawer and pulled out the folder. She showed him the letter she had received from Wilbur, telling her about Eiland von Kuhrt's treachery.

"I have this folder of evidence. Apparently Wilbur was planning to take Von to court so he kept all these papers. He'd even spoken to Don Alo in Pago Pago, but Mr. Alo is not at all interested in handling the case." She handed the folder to Edward Crane. "Here, you can look these papers over while I make us some fresh coffee. Then I'd like to know what you think of all this business." She picked up the pot and went to the kitchen.

When she returned, she found Edward Crane seated at the desk with the papers spread before him. "Tell me, miss, just what did you have in mind?"

"I believe that my uncle was right. Von did get control of this plantation. He managed to somehow with his position on the board of directors at the bank. Anyway I lost my inheritance and I think I should have it back."

Mr. Crane ran blunt fingers through his wiry hair. "And you're ready to go to court?"

"Yes. If I can find a lawyer to represent me. That's what I want from you. Your advice about someone. Don Alo won't do anything."

The older man sipped his coffee. "You're quite a slip of a girl to take on someone as prominent as Eiland von Kuhrt. Aren't you working for him? What'll that do to your job?"

"Oh, I'm sure I'll be fired. Von isn't likely to put up with an employee suing him. That doesn't seem like him."

The New Zealander smiled and shook his head. "No, it isn't. I'm afraid he'd run you off his place."

"Actually I'm expecting him to let me go anytime. We had quite a row the other night, and I told him that he was a thief and I was going to bring him to justice."

"That took a bit of nerve, miss. More than I've got."

"Do you have a good lawyer you could recommend?"

Edward Crane shook his head. "No, Miss Elwood, I don't because I'm going to tell you something that may change your mind. I promised Wilbur on my word of honor that I would never tell anyone, and I haven't, of course. But I'm going to break that promise and I have a feeling that Wilbur would approve. But you're to keep this confidential, because it wouldn't do any good to talk about it. It'd just open up a lot of wounds that have finally healed." He looked slightly nervous.

"Of course I'll keep anything you tell me confidential."

Mr. Crane leaned back in the swivel desk chair. "You knew that Wilbur was an alcoholic?"

"Yes, from what people have told me. I'm sure he was a heavy drinker."

"I'm not blaming him. It's an easy habit to get into

156

out here in the tropics like this, especially when you live alone. And you know, of course, that he was awfully close to both the older Von Kuhrts. Thought a lot of the two of them. Von too before Gunther died."

"I see."

"Well, one day Gunther took Wilbur Elwood with him to Falelumu to meet the freighter. He drove a Land-Rover. Something came on the boat that Von Kuhrt wanted. Anyway old Elwood had been drinking pretty heavy as usual. Soon after they left Falelumu, Gunther said he didn't feel well and he asked Wilbur to take the wheel. He stopped the Land-Rover and they changed places."

A wave of horror washed over Thayer as she realized what was coming. "Oh, no."

Edward Crane nodded "Oh, yes. Wilbur was so drunk, he couldn't manage the Land-Rover around the curves on the grade. He came roaring up the hill, missed the turn, and the Land-Rover flew out into space. He managed to jump out, but poor Gunther didn't."

Thayer whispered, "Oh, how awful!"

"He was dead when they found him at the bottom. Apparently he grabbed at the wheel and tried to save himself. Everyone assumed that he was driving and your uncle let them think so, of course. He was the one that started the story about Gunther having a heart attack."

"And he told you all this?"

"Yes." Crane shook his head sadly. "It nearly drove him crazy. He felt so guilty, he almost lost his mind. He blamed himself entirely. He felt that if he hadn't have been intoxicated that day Gunther would still be alive. And I guess he would be."

Thayer stared at Edward Crane. "That's when Uncle Wilbur began to go downhill. Really got bad, I mean."

"That's right. Acted like a crazy man, he did. Was drunk most of the time. He just couldn't face his guilty conscience, that was the trouble. And he couldn't keep the plantation going. No way. No way at all. Von tried to help Wilbur. Loaned him money. Sent his men and equipment over here to help out. Did everything he could until Wilbur turned against him."

"Then these records of things that Von took away were his in the first place."

"Of course." The New Zealander finished his coffee. "Naturally the directors of the bank were frantic by then. They had overextended themselves terribly with Wilbur. There was no way he could pay his loans. They finally turned Seacrest over to Von to try to salvage something out of the mess. Von can do it if anyone can."

"So that's why Don Alo—"

"Of course, miss. A lawsuit over this would be thrown out of court. No reputable attorney would take on such a case. Von never stole anything from Wilbur, and he has all the records to prove it. He'd make mincemeat out of you if you sued him. So you just forget it, miss, and make your apologies to Von so you'll have a job."

Thayer was reeling at this unexpected news. "How wrong I've been!"

"I think Von suspected all the time that Wilbur was driving and was to blame for his father's death. He might even have accused him at some time. I don't know. But Wilbur turned against Von and there was bad blood between them."

"I know there was."

Edward Crane ran his fingers through his hair again. "Now I'm expecting you to keep this to yourself. Let Mrs. von Kuhrt think her husband had a heart attack at the wheel and was killed. She thought a lot of Wilbur, so what good is it to tell her the truth now? No finer lady ever lived, and she has problems enough with her health so bad."

"You're right. No good would come of it. But how tragic for them all!"

Crane got to his feet and reached for the canvas holder of surveying instruments. "I'd best be getting back to Hibiscus Lagoon. Mrs. von Kuhrt is expecting me for lunch."

Thayer stood up also and walked with him to the front door. "I'm so glad I talked this all over with you, Mr. Crane, and I appreciate your confiding in me. If I'd have gone ahead, I would have been in even worse trouble than I am now." She smiled ruefully. "And that's bad enough, I'm afraid." She glanced at the folder of so-called evidence. "I'm sure poor Uncle Wilbur was beyond the point of using good judgment. He should never have considered this lawsuit in the first place."

"That's right." He put out his hand. "You have my sympathies about losing your uncle. But he's much better off. He was carrying a burden that was too heavy for him. He was a good man and his guilt was just destroying him."

Thayer's throat constricted. "It's all so sad." She shook hands. "I hope I see you again."

"Oh, you will. We all know each other here." As he headed for the station wagon he looked back. "Make your peace with Von, miss. He's a fine man, that one is."

Thayer closed the door and shook her head sadly. She was beyond tears. She felt ill with remorse. Von would never forgive her. Never.

CHAPTER 16

For days Thayer lived with her regret; it was always with her no matter how she tried to push it into the back of her mind. There were times that it seemed to tear her apart.

Over and over she relived her scene with Von. Why had she allowed her anger to possess her until she whipped out with words that she didn't mean at all? Why did she tell Von that she despised him when she truly loved him with all her heart? Why didn't she investigate the situation more thoroughly before she called him a thief and threatened him with a lawsuit?

What poor judgment she had used. When all the time she knew that Wilbur was an alcoholic, she had never once questioned the authenticity of his records. Surely all the license plates of the vehicles would be registered at the government headquarters in Pago Pago. Perhaps just a phone call would have told her that the vehicles belonged to Von. Her common, ordinary sense should have made her realize that Von Kuhrt Enterprises was too prosperous and well established to stoop to stealing from poor old Wilbur. She had acted like a child, making a rash move without thinking out all the consequences.

How could she "make her peace" with Von as Edward Crane advised? Von would have nothing to do with her now. He'd flown back to Apia in Western Samoa to be with Lisa, for her father's life still hung in the balance.

She longed to tell the whole story to Mrs. von Kuhrt but she couldn't do it without revealing the truth about Gunther's death. That wise woman would counsel her and tell her what to do if she knew about this last quarrel between Von and herself. But think of the heartache it would cause if the true circumstances of the fatal accident were known. Nothing would be gained but more sorrow. No, she could turn to no one. She had brought this trouble on herself through her own impulsive actions and she'd have to take the consequences now.

Soon after midnight on Thursday morning the wind wakened her. It whined and whistled around the house, rattled the windows, and scraped a tree branch against her windows. Sleeplessly she lay there and listened to the creaking and groaning of the structure as it was buffeted by the gale.

The orchids! She sat up in bed. The orchids! They never should be subjected to such a wind. She should go and lower the heavy tyrlon shades that were installed inside the lath walls purposely to protect the plants. If she started out now, she feared her arrival at Hibiscus Lagoon at this hour would arouse everyone and frighten Mrs. von Kuhrt. She decided to wait until daylight.

The minutes dragged by as the wind seemed to gain in force and hammer at the glass windowpanes, rattling and shaking the house to the very foundation. She tried not to think what was happening to her beautiful orchids.

Finally, before dawn, she climbed out of bed, and pulled on a clean pair of jeans and a yellow top. She braided her dark hair into two pigtails to keep it from whipping across her face. Then she ran downstairs, ate a bowl of cereal, and left a note for Fetu. Before she went outside, she tied a yellow scarf over her hair.

The air seemed heavy and oppressing. She had never

161

experienced that sensation before, as if the air was no longer gaseous but had substance that actually pushed against a person. As she drove toward Hibiscus Lagoon the force of the wind hit against the side of the VW and swerved it to the other edge of the road. Her car was much too light to withstand the force of this blow. She should have driven a truck in such a gale, she realized worriedly. But hers was the only car on the road and she could use the whole surface to go with the gusts that threatened to turn it over. Somehow she managed to keep the small vehicle upright as she crawled along cautiously, not adding great speed to the whipping turbulence around her. If one tree toppled, the little car would be crushed like a matchbox with her in it. Finally she drove into her usual parking spot near the greenhouses.

When she ran inside, she found several pots tipped over. She'd come none too soon, for the damage to the plants would increase with the velocity of the gales. One by one she lowered the heavy shades and fastened them to hooks at the bottom. Then to keep them from whipping, she slipped metal bars across them and fitted the ends into brackets on each side. She had to climb up a ladder to get the top bars in position.

When she heard a noise, she looked down from her perch and saw Von standing there. "Good for you!" he exclaimed. "I just flew over from Apia and stopped to check on these orchids first thing. Such a terrible blow could break them all to pieces."

"The wind woke me up and I came as soon as I could so I could protect the plants."

"Fine. I can't tell you how much I appreciate that. We're catching the edge of a willy-nilly."

"Willy-nilly?"

"Typhoon to you. It's already struck the Solomon

and Santa Cruz islands. I heard the warning on the midnight news in Apia so I left as soon as it was daylight. I'm going to round up my men; we have a lot to do before the full force hits us."

"What can I do to help?"

"Put as many of the plants as you can on the ground under the benches. Call Taligi and Lua and tell them to stay home. And you'd better put your car in the shed."

"Will do."

"Then would you go up to the house and stay with Mother? She gets awfully upset during a typhoon. She worries about all the animals and the people on the island. Maybe you can keep her calm." He hurried to the door. "Thanks for getting here so early, Thayer."

As she watched him step outside and brace himself against the wind, her heart lightened. At least Von had spoken to her. The ice was broken. He'd said nothing about their angry quarrel. She struggled to put the heavy ladder back in its allotted space, then she placed as many of the orchid plants as she could on the ground under the protection of the benches. There was nothing to do but leave the hanging orchids in place and hope for the best.

When she was finished, she headed for the house, gasping for breath in the hammering air as she was buffeted along the path. When she let herself in the side door, only Mrs. von Kuhrt and Tupuasa were in the big house.

The older woman looked up from the breakfast-room table. "Oh, my dear, I didn't expect to see you! Tupuasa and I have sent the rest of the staff home. We're here by ourselves, feeling awfully sorry for us."

Thayer kissed Mrs. von Kuhrt and greeted the housekeeper. "I have special instructions from Von to keep you out of mischief."

"Von? Is he back?" His mother sighed with relief as she put down a glass of orange juice. "Oh, thank God he got here safely. And he'll take charge of everything."

"I saw him before six this morning. I got here around five to lower the shades in the greenhouse to protect the orchids from this wind. I lay in bed last night, visualizing them all blown over and broken. Anyway Von had heard about the typhoon on the news so he flew in as soon as he had some light. He was going to round up his men to do what they could to prevent more damage."

"There's lots they can do. They anchor the big farm machinery down with ropes. Close things up. Get as much as they can under cover. Herd the animals into a protected place. In the village they will rope down all the thatched roofs. By the middle of the afternoon we'll really feel the full force of this."

Tupuasa stood at the kitchen counter, cracking eggs in a bowl. "Would you like some breakfast, Miss Elwood? I'm making an omelet for Mrs. von Kuhrt and myself. I can easily add a few more eggs for you."

"Yes, I would. I'm starved."

Mrs. von Kuhrt patted the table. "Get the mats and silver from the buffet and set places for the three of us. We'll all feel better when we've had a good breakfast."

As Thayer found the silverware she said, "This storm is a new experience for me. I've never been in a typhoon before."

"Well, in Minnesota you must have experienced cyclones. And a typhoon is a tropical cyclone that blows over the water. In the Caribbean they're called hurricanes, of course. In the Philippines they're *baguio* and in Japan *repus* and along the Arabian coast they're known as *asifa-t*."

"Von called it a willy-nilly."

164

"That's what the Aussies say. Whatever it's called in various parts of the world, it adds up to a very destructive windstorm. You'd better plan to stay here all night, dear. Don't try to go home and be in that house alone."

"Thanks, I will stay. Even before five o'clock I barely made it here. I was afraid my VW would be blown right off the road. The wind is lots stronger now."

"It will last for hours and gets more terrifying all the time. Better call Fetu while the lines are still up. If she knows you're staying here she won't worry. She and Tofilau can go back to their house for the duration."

After breakfast Tupuasa announced that she was going to prepare dinner ahead while she still had electricity and then she could warm it on a kerosene stove. She put candles in each of the rooms with a box of matches near each holder. "You never know how long we'll have lights," she explained.

Mrs. von Kuhrt took Thayer into the luxurious sitting room of her downstairs wing. They played gin rummy to keep their minds off the creaking house, the rattling windows, and the strange, terrifying roar outside. But all the time Thayer thought of Von. She knew that Mrs. von Kuhrt was terribly worried too.

Finally Tupuasa came. "It's time for you to go in your Jacuzzi, Mrs. von Kuhrt."

The older woman put down her cards. "Well, anyway I won this game." She looked around uneasily. "I do hope Von is all right. I wish he'd come home."

"He's fine, I'm sure," Thayer said with an assurance she didn't feel. She tried not to show her own concern for she knew only too well what it meant to battle the force of the wind. A vehicle could capsize, an animal go beserk and attack him, or a building collapse on him. Almost anything could happen in such a storm. "Shall I

165

use the same guest room upstairs that I had before?" she asked, rising.

Tupuasa answered, "Yes, use the same room. I'll get your bed ready later."

"No, I'll make it now. I haven't anything else to do. Where do I find some sheets?"

"There's a linen closet near the head of the stairs, Miss Elwood."

"If I had been smart, I would have brought an overnight bag with my nightgown and toilet articles."

"You'll find extra gowns and things in the dresser drawer of that guest room, also some caftans, when you want to change."

Thayer climbed the stairs, found the linen, and went into the room she'd occupied previously. When the bed was made, she stood at the window to look outside.

Beyond the reef, wind-carved ocean waves heaved and tumbled under white foam crests. Instead of the usual emerald green or vivid blue color, the sea had turned into a black, churning mass that tossed tons and tons of water into the air only to crash down again. It was a nightmarish cauldron of angry, heaving water.

As she listened to the wind hammer at the house and batter at the windows, she thought of what Mrs. von Kuhrt had told her about how many fish seem to sense the approach of a typhoon. As the barometer drops the fish bite greedily and some, like the bluefish, deliberately swim to the bottom to gobble small stones and gravel to act as ballast to keep them on the ocean floor.

But the birds must suffer most of all in such a storm, Thayer thought. As the winds begin to swing in a vortex, surely they would be caught helplessly in the maelström. Some would be battered against the cliffs along the coast. Perhaps the shore birds could crawl into cracks and crevices to find refuge from the tumult.

As Thayer stood there, the wind grew stronger and built to an enormous horrifying sound. She gasped for breath as the air pressure crushed down on her, becoming denser by its own weight.

Why didn't Von come home? His welfare was more important than buildings or plantation equipment. If she only knew that he was safe! Anxiously she watched the wind-lashed palms writhe and twist. Perhaps he was waiting in one of the other buildings until the storm subsided. But why didn't he phone? Surely he would know that they'd be worried. Usually he was so considerate of his mother. Perhaps the lines had been blown down.

Too nervous to read or lie down, she paced the floor, trying to keep her mind off the mounting crescendo. Restlessly she moved back and forth and then returned to the window to look out. That was very dangerous to do, she knew, for the glass could blow in. But she looked out on the other side of the lawn area toward the headquarters buildings.

Finally she saw a figure on the pathway. It was Von, bent double, struggling against the force of the wind. Oh, thank God! At least he was safe. But he took a step only to be forced back. He turned with his back to the gale and tried to walk backward. "Come on, come on," she urged. She watched him inch toward the house, then stagger drunkenly as a thrust hit him. He stumbled, nearly fell down.

It was agony to watch him fight the force of the storm. He faltered back and forth across the path, struggling valiantly with all his strength. A terrific gust hit him and he fell prone, facedown, his arms and legs stretched out.

"Are you hurt, darling? Oh, are you hurt?" she cried aloud from the window.

167

The branches of a thirty-foot tropical almond with large leathery leaves bent low over the pathway as the wind battered against it and then it sprang back into place. With the spread of the branches he would have twenty feet of protection from the worst of the onslaughts. "Get to the tree."

Finally he pulled himself up until he was on all fours. He crawled on his hands and knees inch by inch. Finally he was under the tree, which took the brunt of the wind. He stood up, bent over as if to offer as little resistance as possible, and moved toward the house. Just as he reached the trunk, the gale racketed against the biggest branch, tore it loose, and rammed it on top of Von's bent figure, throwing him to the ground.

Thayer screamed in horror. "Oh, God! He'll be killed!"

CHAPTER 17

Thayer grabbed her scarf, tied it around her head, and flew down the stairs. She found Tupuasa in the kitchen.

"Telephone for help right away! I saw a tree branch crash down on Von! He's on the path outside. Try to find some men to help me."

She ran for the door and pushed with all her might to open it against the force of the wind. It was sheltered enough in the deep doorway to finally give way until she could wriggle through the opening. Then she began her fight to get to Von. Gusts of wind and rain battered her face until she was hardly able to see. The gale roared around her, clawed at her scarf, billowed her shirt behind her until she staggered backward. Finally she dropped on her hands and knees and crawled on the wet grass toward the tree.

She sobbed as she inched her way toward the fallen branch over Von. "Oh, dear God, don't let him be killed!"

Branches slapped in the air, wires screamed, and the wind whistled around her, creating a pandemonium clamor of sound that swelled and lessened with change in force. The rain pounded on her back; pebbles and sand bit into her knees and the palms of her hands; tears ran down her cheeks.

Finally she reached the tree and saw Von facedown under a canopy of leathery leaves, pinned to the ground by the great branch crushed on top of him. He lay terribly still, not moving at all.

"Oh, Von! Oh, my darling!" she sobbed, as she tried to push the branch away. She strained and yanked but she couldn't budge it.

Finally she parted the entangled branches and crawled through them, the twigs gouging and scratching her back. Wet leaves slapped against her face. Painfully she worked her way toward Von. When she was near, she saw blood gushing from a deep gash on the inside of his thigh, forming a red stream that bypassed and circled around the twigs and finally mingled with the rain pool on the path.

"Von! Dearest Von!" she whimpered in panic. She had to do something at once. He'd bleed to death if she didn't act promptly. Apply pressure, that was the first step. She reached between his legs, tried to find a spot where the pressure would stop the flow of blood. But nothing helped. The blood poured from the cut.

She frantically tried to remember what she'd learned in the first-aid course she had taken in university. First she found a short, strong branch and bent and twisted it until it was loosened from the limb. She managed to break off a piece.

There wasn't a moment to lose. Tears of panic flooded her eyes but she wiped her face on her wet sleeve. Hurriedly she yanked her scarf off her head and stuffed one end under Von's leg. She managed to lift his leg enough so she could reach under his thigh from the other side, grab hold of the scarf, and pull it around.

Finally she had the scarf in position above the wound, so she tied it into a half-knot and placed the stick in the center, then tied the ends securely around it into a full knot. Now the stick could act like a windlass. As she twisted it around and around, the tourniquet tightened. She secured the stick into place by tying the ends of the scarf to the fallen limb. Gradually the flow of blood diminished until it was only a trickle. It would be safe to leave the tourniquet in place for at least an hour.

She pushed leaves away from Von's ashen face and saw blood ooze from his mouth and nose. She took the bottom of her shirt and gently wiped the blood away. Von was unconscious but he was alive! She slumped against the branch, almost weak with relief.

Every few minutes Thayer loosened the tourniquet to allow the blood to circulate in Von's leg. But as the blood began to flow out of the wound she tightened the stick windlass again. Nervously she peered through the overhanging branches and leaves to see if help was coming. She hoped Tupuasa was able to reach someone. Was the telephone still in operation? Von ought to be inside and dry. But at least he was lying still and she'd stopped the hemorrhaging.

The wind howled around them. The tree shuddered and bent low with its force and then shook the surrounding ground as it snapped back into place. They were in the shelter of the trunk but it was a dangerous spot too, for if the entire tree came down they would be killed.

She looked at Von's white face, then put her hand on his chest and felt his rapid, weak heartbeat. He was in shock. Did he have a brain concussion? Were any bones fractured? Were there internal injuries? Could he survive a flight to the hospital in Pago Pago? She murmured a prayer for help, as she needed some soon.

Finally she saw four big men coming from the headquarters building, carrying a stretcher, saws, and axes. They bent low to keep their heads down from the force of the gale, although it seemed less violent at the moment. As they struggled near she untied the ends of the scarf from the branch and held the stick windlass on the tourniquet with her hand.

171

As they approached, Thayer called, "Right in here! This limb is pinning him down."

One man seemed to take charge. He shouted, "Not to worry, miss. We'll get the boss out of there okay." He gave directions to the others where to saw off the fallen limb.

Soon the branch was cut in pieces and enough of it taken away so that the men could place the stretcher next to Von and carefully lift him onto it. While she held the tourniquet, they struggled to the house during a lull in the storm.

Tupuasa met them at the door and held it open. "There's a couch in Mr. von Kuhrt's study. We'll put him there. I have it all ready." She closed the door and led the way.

While Von was still on the stretcher, Tupuasa got a big pair of shears and cut his clothes away, then patted him dry.

Finally the men expertly lifted Von from the stretcher and placed him on the couch. The man in charge warned, "Don't use any pillows. Not with his face so white. He may have a skull fracture." He examined the wound and said, "His blood is beginning to coagulate so we won't need the tourniquet. I'll sterilize his wound and put a bandage on it." He reached for the first-aid materials on the tray that Tupuasa had prepared.

When he finished, Thayer covered Von with a sheet and light blanket. She said to the men, "You knew just how to handle Mr. von Kuhrt. Thank you so much."

"We're the rescue squad for this end of the island," one of the men said proudly. "The boss had the Red Cross come and train us."

The one in charge said, "We can't get through to Pago Pago by telephone but we already reached the

Red Cross by ham radio. They'll send an ambulance plane for the injured as soon as they can get through. Others here on the island have been hurt too. But the plane can't come until the worst of the storm is over. That may be tomorrow morning."

Thayer said, "We'll take care of him the best we can. At least he'll be warm and dry and absolutely quiet."

Tupuasa asked, "Did the typhoon hit all of Samoa?"

"No, mostly Nanotuma and Swains Island. We're the farthest north. Guess we caught the edge of the blow as it left the Santa Cruz Islands," the leader answered. "We have to go now; we have other calls to make."

As Thayer walked with them to the door she said, "Thank God you came when you did. We can't thank you enough."

When the rescue squad was gone, Thayer turned to Tupuasa and asked, "Does Mrs. von Kuhrt know?"

Tupuasa shook her head. "No, she's been taking a nap." Her face crumbled and she started to cry.

Thayer patted her shoulder. "I'll stay with Von. But as soon as you hear his mother moving around let me know. I'll tell her about the accident and bring her in here."

"Do you think he'll live?"

"Yes, I do." She dropped to her knees and felt his wrist. "He's unconscious but I think his pulse is stronger than it was. He's badly injured, of course. But at least he's out of the storm and safe. We'll keep him perfectly quiet and do all we can until the ambulance plane comes."

"I'll go see if Mrs. von Kuhrt is awake now," Tupuasa offered.

Soon she returned and said, "Yes, she's up. I'll stay with Mr. Von if you'll go to her. I'm afraid I'll cry."

Thayer swallowed the lump in her throat. "I'll try not

to." She looked down at Von. "His color is better now. At least we can get comfort from that. I'll go to his mother now."

Before she lost her courage she hurried to Mrs. von Kuhrt's sitting room and found her already in her wheelchair ready to come out for tea.

Thayer put her arm across the older woman's shoulder and said gently, "Darling, Von has had an accident but he's going to be all right." She told the whole story of the rescue and said, "I'm going to take you to his study so you can be with him."

When Mrs. von Kuhrt saw him, she gasped and broke down. Thayer held her close and let her cry. "He's going to be all right. His color is much better and his pulse is stronger. Of course he's in shock now but he'll pull through."

Tupuasa hovered anxiously nearby. "They reached the Red Cross in Pago Pago by ham radio. They'll send an ambulance plane as soon as they can."

In a few minutes they were all under control and Thayer said, "Tupuasa, would you please make a pot of tea for us? Bring yourself a cup too, and we'll have it here."

When the housekeeper left, Mrs. von Kuhrt whispered, "Wasn't it fortunate that you were looking out the window when the limb fell on him? He could have been out there for hours and no one would have known."

"That's right. Those big leaves on that tropical almond covered him completely." Thayer shuddered as she traced the flowers on the caftan that she had put on. Von could have bled to death if she hadn't known he was there. "I'm going to look at his wound and see if I need to reapply the tourniquet. But it's only supposed to be used temporarily."

She reached under the sheet, loosened the bandage,

174

and watched for signs of bleeding, but there were none. Apparently the blood was clotting all right.

Mrs. von Kuhrt cried, "Thank God, Thayer, that you were here. You saved his life."

The long vigil began. They had their tea, then later supper in the dining room while they listened for news on the transistor radio. It was true that only Nanotuma and Swains Island in the Samoa group were in the path of the typhoon.

Later Thayer insisted that she would sit up with Von all night while Mrs. von Kuhrt and Tupuasa slept. "As soon as the ambulance plane arrives tomorrow and picks up Von, I'll go to bed and spend the day there."

Finally she settled herself in a comfortable chair by the side of Von's couch. She had to be near him in case the bleeding started again from his nose or the wound. She felt his pulse and put her hand on his chest. His heartbeat was slower and stronger, which was a good sign.

As the hours slowly passed she was grateful to be alone with Von. She looked at his dear face in the muted light, put her hand over his, and murmured aloud, "I love you, darling, with all my heart. I know you can't hear me but I want to tell you anyway. I'm sorry for the things I said. They weren't true at all. I was angry and said things I didn't mean. Forgive me."

Tears streamed down her cheeks. Tomorrow Von would be flown to the hospital in Pago Pago where he would no doubt regain consciousness. Lisa would come, and he would be hers.

But she had saved his life and for a few short hours he was hers alone. She took a washcloth and dampened it with water from a pitcher. Then she wiped his face and hands. She studied each feature to stamp them indelibly on her memory. She might have to leave Samoa

175

but at least she could take her mental impressions with her.

"I love you, dearest Von. I know the truth now. I should never have doubted you," she rambled on. "I should have known the confused impressions of an alcoholic. Poor Uncle Wilbur could not face the truth about himself and Seacrest. He had to find someone else to blame, and you were chosen, of course. You were right and I was so mistaken. Forgive me. Please forgive me, for I love you so very much."

All through the night she talked to him as if to purge herself of all her regrets and heartaches. This would be her last time alone with him. She wanted to tell him how she felt even though she knew he couldn't hear her.

CHAPTER 18

At daybreak Tupuasa came to the study. "Now I will stay with Mr. Von. You must go get some rest. I insist."

Thayer stood up, almost shaking with fatigue. She made one last check on Von. He seemed a little better; his heartbeat was definitely stronger and his color more normal.

"All right, I will go rest." But first she went to the window and looked out. The storm had abated. Although the wind was still blowing, it was not of typhoon velocity. "I'm sure a plane can make it from Pago Pago."

"I think so too. You rest and I'll call you as soon as the doctor comes."

When her head hit the pillow, she fell asleep. It seemed only a few minutes later before Tupuasa shook her awake.

"Miss Elwood, wake up! The doctor is here."

Thayer sat up in bed. "I'll come down right away. What time is it?"

"Ten o'clock. The doctor is examining Mr. Von, and I know he'll want to talk to you." Before Tupuasa left, she pointed to Thayer's jeans, yellow shirt, and underclothing folded over a chair. "I washed and dried your clothes so you'd have them to put on."

"Thank you, Tupuasa. No wonder Mrs. von Kuhrt calls you a jewel! How is she this morning?"

"She had a poor night but she feels better now that the doctor is here."

Thayer climbed out of bed, took a quick shower, and slipped into her clothes as fast as possible. She brushed her hair, braided it into pigtails again, and hurried down the stairs.

A Samoan doctor and nurse were in the study with Von so she waited outside the door. Mrs. von Kuhrt saw her so she pushed the wheels of her chair across the room and joined her in the hallway.

"Von regained consciousness," his mother said, her face attesting to her sleepless night. "The doctor definitely feels he can stand the flight all right."

"Good. Does he know how badly Von is injured?"

"Not really. He says no one can tell until they take X rays and make a complete examination at the hospital."

Thayer patted Mrs. von Kuhrt's shoulder. "Well, at least it's a relief to know that he's under medical care. That's worth everything."

"Yes, and the fact that he's strong enough to be moved."

The doctor came out into the hallway, and after Mrs. von Kuhrt introduced them, he said, "Your quick thinking saved Mr. von Kuhrt's life, I'm sure of that. He could have bled to death. He's fortunate that you saw the limb go down. Not only that, but he got excellent emergency care until we could come."

"Thank you, Doctor."

"We landed on your airstrip, Mrs. von Kuhrt. As soon as the other injured people are loaded onto the plane, the rescue squad will come and get your son. Then we'll leave for Pago Pago immediately. I'll call your own doctor to take over the case, of course."

Mrs. von Kuhrt touched his arm. "Could you have the doctor telephone us as soon as he has a report?"

"Certainly."

The rescue squad arrived soon and carried Von on a

stretcher to a panel truck converted to an ambulance for the ride to the plane.

When they were alone, Mrs. von Kuhrt said, "Thayer, will you stay here with me while Von is gone?"

"Of course I will. It will be a difficult time for you. I'll go check on my orchids now. Then later today I'll go home and pack some clothes."

"Thank you, dear. I just want you here with me. You're such a comfort. Just think what might've happened if you hadn't been here yesterday." Her chin quivered and she pressed her cheek against Thayer's hand.

"Well, I was here." She kissed the older woman's cheek. "I have to see how my poor orchids are, so I'm going."

"I'd like to come with you but I don't feel up to it. I think I'll go back to bed until lunchtime."

The usually flawless grounds of Hibiscus Lagoon looked like a battleground. Broken branches, fallen limbs, palm fronds, and leaves were scattered all over the lawn. As she approached the plantation headquarters she could see more damage. Roofs were off some of the smaller buildings, and various sheds were completely blown over.

Since the orchid greenhouses were protected by other buildings, they didn't get the full thrust of the wind and were still upright. However some of the hanging orchids were crashed to the ground and lay broken in bits. She would have to estimate their value for insurance purposes. But at that, they were lucky to have survived so well. She didn't expect Taligi and Lua to come so she cleaned up the damage herself.

Later she reported to Mrs. von Kuhrt at the lunch table. "But we were fortunate at that. We could have lost all the orchids and the buildings too."

"It was the fact that you were there so early to pull the curtains down, Thayer. You've been very conscientious with your work, and Von appreciates that."

"Have you heard anything yet?"

"No, but Lisa called. It seems that the telephone service has been restored. I was hoping the call was about Von, but it was Lisa and she wanted to know how we survived the typhoon. When I told her about Von, she said she'd fly to Pago Pago as soon as possible." Mrs. von Kuhrt made a face.

Thayer laughed to cover her aching jealousy. "I knew she'd go."

"I wish the typhoon would blow her away so we'd never see her around here again."

"It won't, I'm afraid. But the wind's not so bad now. I think I'll go home to Seacrest and get some clothes. I want to see what damage is done there."

"Your house faces the bay, which helps. We get the wind here right off the ocean."

Everywhere Thayer looked on the road to Seacrest showed the effects of the typhoon. Buildings were leveled; fences, down; trees, uprooted. She tried to see the Seacrest fields as she drove along.

Fortunately the gray house had survived the gales and she greeted it like an old friend. Fetu and Tofilau came running out the back door, surrounded by barking dogs.

She greeted her two Samoan helpers. "I'm so glad you're all right."

Fetu asked, "What about Mr. Von? Tupuasa called early this morning and told us about him."

As they walked into the kitchen Thayer gave a report. Then she added, "Mrs. von Kuhrt wants me to stay with her so I'm going to pack some clothes. I'll let you know when I'll be back."

"Well, we'll spend our time cleaning up the yard," Tofilau said as he sat at the breakfast table. "Everything's a mess. It'll take weeks to get it back to normal."

They talked awhile and then Thayer went up to her room and got out her suitcase. She tried to keep her mind on the things she wanted to take, but all she could think about was Von.

When she returned to Hibiscus Lagoon, Mrs. von Kuhrt was full of news. She looked so much better that Thayer knew that the report had been a hopeful one.

"Well, Von's going to pull through. Dr. Tamasese called and he'd just read all the X rays. Some internal injuries but they will heal. There is a concussion but no serious skull fracture. No other fractures. The thigh wound needs some surgery, which they will perform this evening. The doctor thought he'd be in the hospital for about ten days and then he could come home with a nurse."

"Well, what a relief! It could be so much worse." Thayer plunked her suitcase on the floor and slumped into a chair. "We'll all sleep tonight."

"You must be dead on your feet, dear. No sleep last night and only a little this morning."

"I'll take a nap now and see you at dinner. We can have a wild game of gin rummy later."

The next day the storm was over and things were back to normal. The household staff all reported to work, Taligi and Lua arrived at the orchid greenhouse, and the gardeners began to clean the debris and broken branches off of the lawn.

The two Samoan women were full of talk of the storm damage as all of them raised the shades, put the orchids back in their proper place, and cleaned the layer of dust off the worktables.

Taligi gave Thayer a knowing look. "We heard how you saved Mr. Von's life, how you risked your own safety to go out in the typhoon to help him. The *matai* says that proves that the gods sent you here. You were the one meant to keep him alive."

"Oh, no. I just happened to see the branch fall when I was standing near a window." Mixed emotions of amusement and annoyance ran through Thayer. Nothing happened on this island that wasn't thoroughly talked about in the village.

At lunchtime Mrs. von Kuhrt said, "I talked to Von this morning. He said he has sandbags around his head to hold it in one position. His thigh hurts and so does his rib cage, but actually he sounded pretty good. He wants you to call him at seven o'clock tonight; he wants to thank you personally for all you did for him."

All afternoon she anticipated talking to Von. How she looked forward to the call—to hearing his voice again. She dreamed of what she would say to him and how he would answer back. Perhaps she could even ask his forgiveness and have that behind her before he came home. When the time finally came, her hand trembled as she dialed. Her heart thrashed around when she reached the hospital and asked for his number.

A woman answered and Thayer asked, "May I speak to Mr. von Kuhrt?"

"Of course, Thayer. This is Lisa. I guess you didn't recognize my voice. I flew over late this afternoon to be with Von. He was so surprised."

Thayer's heart sank with disappointment. Lisa was there already. When Von came on the phone, his voice was formal and guarded. "Both my mother and the doctors tell me that I owe you a vote of thanks. But how do you thank someone who has saved your life?"

"I just happened to be at the right place at the right time. I was looking out an upstairs window when I saw the limb come down on you. It was just luck that I was there."

182

"Well, thank you, Thayer. It was certainly lucky for me. I'm going to order a memento and bring it home with me so you'll have something to remember this experience by."

They talked a few more minutes, and then his voice sounded tired.

"I'd better hang up, Von. It's wonderful to hear your voice."

"Thank you for staying with Mother, and give her my love." His words sounded so stiff and unnatural.

When she replaced the phone, tears swam in her eyes and rolled unheeded down her cheeks. She loved him. She loved him wholeheartedly. But Lisa was with him now and would be always. There was no place for her in Von's life.

She thought back over the conversation. He had been polite, but there was no warmth. Naturally he would want to thank her for saving his life, but it was obvious that he hadn't forgiven her.

While she was still by the telephone, it rang again, so she answered it and heard Russell's voice. "Thayer! I've been trying to get you ever since I heard about the storm. There's no answer at Seacrest so I called Von for news."

"Well, a lot has happened." She told him about the storm, Von's accident, and his being in the hospital.

"I'll go see him tomorrow. I'm glad he isn't in worse shape."

They talked awhile longer, and finally she replaced the receiver and thought sadly, "What a mix-up. We're all in love with the wrong people."

She thought about how Russell would feel when she refused his proposal. He had spoken several times of a girl in California. Whether she was his girl-friend before Thayer she didn't know, but perhaps he could turn to her for solace.

The days went by, and soon it was time for Von to come home. The household was in a stir, preparing for his arrival with the nurse. No doubt Lisa would come in the same plane with them.

At noon Thayer packed her clothes and told Mrs. von Kuhrt, "Von comes home tomorrow so you'll have plenty of company. I'm going home after work."

"I wish you could stay here all the time but I know you're anxious to return home, of course. You were such a dear to help me through all this."

Thayer waited until the day after Von arrived to stop by the big house after work. Mrs. von Kuhrt was on the terrace, and she waved her over. "Von's asleep now but he wants to see you. Why don't you have dinner here, then you can see him when he's rested?"

"Fine. I'll just run home and shower and change." She didn't want Lisa to see her looking rumpled in her work clothes anyway. She kissed Mrs. von Kuhrt and said, "See you later."

"We'll eat about eight. But you come for a drink with Von about seven. He has a little gift for you."

Maybe it was a charm on a gold bracelet, she thought as she climed into her VW. Something with waves and a bent palm tree. Something to remember her life here in Samoa when she had to leave. Would she ever be able to wear it? Wouldn't it be too heartbreaking to have a reminder of this paradise that she'd found and was to leave all too soon?

Since she had nearly two hours to get ready, she took her time. She showered, shampooed her hair, and blew it dry so that it framed her face in soft waves. She applied eye makeup and lipstick. Then she put on her pale green jersey sheath that she'd worn the first night of her stay at Hibiscus Lagoon. What a lot had happened since then. Well, she was completing the circle, for Von was probably going to thank her, give her a gift, and

184

ask her to leave. Perhaps it was all for the best, as it would be too painful to stay and see Von and Lisa together.

When she arrived at Hibiscus Lagoon, there was no sign of Mrs. von Kuhrt or Lisa. No doubt Her Highness was getting dressed to make one of her grand entrances, or perhaps she was already with Von. A maid ushered her upstairs to his master bedroom with great windows that looked out at the sea. It was the first time she'd ever been in his room, and she felt a little shy as she crossed the floor to where he lay in bed. She took a deep breath to calm herself. He looked as handsome as ever in his white silk pajamas.

"Hi. How are you, Von?"

"Okay."

She dropped in the chair beside his bed and looked around. "Where is Lisa? I expected to see her here." Relief flooded through her. At least she would have privacy for her little speech of apology that she had prepared.

"She had to return to Apia." He turned his head carefully so he could see her. There were no pillows, only sandbags as support. "How beautiful you look, Thayer."

"Thank you, Von." Her voice sounded stilted. How could she begin her speech? "Your mother was kind enough to ask me for dinner. She told me that you wanted me to come now." She seemed to be throwing words out, playing for time.

"That's right. But scoot your chair closer. I'm not supposed to raise my head without the nurse helping me."

She moved her chair against the bed and put her hand on the sheet. How she longed to touch him, to caress his pale face, to push away from his eyebrows the lock of hair that had fallen forward, to kiss his lips.

185

Von went on. "My nurse is having her dinner downstairs now. That's why I wanted you to come at this time." He looked at her for a long moment, then put his hand over hers, "Thayer, the night I was injured I had the strangest dream. I was half conscious but I heard your voice. I couldn't reply. But it seemed that you were talking to me."

Color flooded over her face. He had heard her! She had bared her soul to him, thinking that he was unconscious and unable to hear her.

Von continued, "You told me over and over that you loved me. Oh, my darling, I hope it wasn't a dream!" He pulled her hand to his mouth and kissed her palm. "I hope it wasn't just a dream, for I've loved you for a long, long time."

She could hardly believe what she was hearing. Finally she whispered, "It wasn't a dream. I did talk to you, but I had no idea you could hear me. Oh, Von, I've loved you for a long time too."

"But I thought it was you and Russell!"

"And I thought it was you and Lisa!"

He kissed her hand again. "What fools we were. All this time there's been a special magic between us."

"I've loved you from the very first. So perhaps the gods did send me." Tears flooded her eyes, but she blinked them away.

"Lean over so I can kiss you, dearest. I can't lift my head."

She kissed him and he put his arm around her neck and held her close. "When I get well, I'll do a lot better than that." He laughed a little shakily. "This is a hell of a way to propose when I'm in bed like this, but will you marry me, darling?"

For a moment she couldn't speak. The words wouldn't come. Finally she managed, "Oh, Von, of course I will." She wiped the tears away with the back of her hand. "Isn't this crazy? I thought you were going to fire me. I never expected a proposal."

"Fire you? Why that never entered my mind!" he chuckled.

She sat on the edge of his bed and held him. "I can't wait to tell your mother!"

Her chin quivered and tears spilled over. "I'm so happy, I'm crying."

"I could too." He held her hand. "But mine are tears of frustration that I have to lie so still when I want so much more."

"Oh, dearest, you'll soon be well and then—"

"Then I'll make up for lost time, you can depend on that," he finished. He reached under his pillow and brought out a little jewel box. "This is the memento I promised." He opened the case and took out the most magnificent diamond engagement ring she'd ever seen. He held her hand and slipped the ring on her finger. "It fits! What a miracle!"

She held her hand up and the ring caught the light and burst into a thousand fiery prisms of brightness. "It's so very, very beautiful! I've never seen anything so lovely!" She turned her hand in all directions to admire the ring's magnificence. "But how did you buy it? When? You were in the hospital."

"We have a jeweler in Pago Pago. He came to the hospital when I sent for him and brought all his catalogs. We ordered the ring from New York, and it came by air. The jeweler delivered it to me day before yesterday. Just in time."

"I can't believe it." She smiled. "I was sure you were going to give me a charm on a bracelet." She looked at him lovingly, allowing herself the luxury of showing her emotion.

187

"Von, when did you know that you loved me?"

"Remember when you were explaining pollination to my mother in the greenhouse? I came in and objected, and you tore into me like a wounded tiger. Wow! But you were so genuinely devoted to Mother and wanted the best for her—that's when I first began to suspect. I love your passion and your compassion."

"And I thought all the time that you'd marry Lisa."

"I never asked her, but I'll admit I considered it many times. Her music completely enthralls me. That's why I had her come to visit. I wanted to see the two of you together and be sure of my feelings for you."

Thayer considered the wonderful change in her life.

"And I thought I belonged at Seacrest. . . . I love it there, but I'll gladly give it up for you."

"Speaking of Seacrest—I have big ideas for that place. While I lay in the hospital, I made all kinds of plans. I'd like to pay off the bank and take the whole operation over in my name and yours and start from scratch. Mike Snyder would be perfect for the job as manager. He could also serve as my assistant for all my properties," he continued enthusiastically. "He and Judy Rhinehart will be married later and could live in your house. You might like to have a girl your own age around."

"How marvelous that will be! I like Judy very much."

"Then that's settled. Let's get married when your parents come in October. Is that okay? I ought to be recovered by then."

She nodded. "That would be perfect." She leaned down and kissed him.

"We'll have to be married down by the lagoon," he said. "Everyone on the whole island will want to come to the wedding—all the Samoans as well as the planters."

188

"I particularly want the Samoans from the village. They have all been rooting for me instead of Lisa." They both laughed, gazing warmly into each other's eyes.

Gradually their smiles faded, and Thayer felt a rush of tenderness for him. But Von was the first to say, "I love you."

Love—the way you want it!

Candlelight Romances

		TITLE NO.	
☐ A MAN OF HER CHOOSING by Nina Pykare	$1.50	#554	(15133-3)
☐ PASSING FANCY by Mary Linn Roby	$1.50	#555	(16770-1)
☐ THE DEMON COUNT by Anne Stuart	$1.25	#557	(11906-5)
☐ WHERE SHADOWS LINGER by Janis Susan May	$1.25	#556	(19777-5)
☐ OMEN FOR LOVE by Esther Boyd	$1.25	#552	(16108-8)
☐ MAYBE TOMORROW by Marie Pershing	$1.25	#553	(14909-6)
☐ LOVE IN DISGUISE by Nina Pykare	$1.50	#548	(15229-1)
☐ THE RUNAWAY HEIRESS by Lillian Cheatham	$1.50	#549	(18083-X)
☐ HOME TO THE HIGHLANDS by Jessica Eliot	$1.25	#550	(13104-9)
☐ DARK LEGACY by Candace Connell	$1.25	#551	(11771-2)
☐ LEGACY OF THE HEART by Lorena McCourtney	$1.25	#546	(15645-9)
☐ THE SLEEPING HEIRESS by Phyllis Taylor Pianka	$1.50	#543	(17551-8)
☐ DAISY by Jennie Tremaine	$1.50	#542	(11683-X)
☐ RING THE BELL SOFTLY by Margaret James	$1.25	#545	(17626-3)
☐ GUARDIAN OF INNOCENCE by Judy Boynton	$1.25	#544	(11862-X)
☐ THE LONG ENCHANTMENT by Helen Nuelle	$1.25	#540	(15407-3)
☐ SECRET LONGINGS by Nancy Kennedy	$1.25	#541	(17609-3)

At your local bookstore or use this handy coupon for ordering:

Dell DELL BOOKS
P.O. BOX 1000, PINEBROOK, N.J. 07058

Please send me the books I have checked above. I am enclosing $ _____
(please add 75¢ per copy to cover postage and handling). Send check or money order—no cash or C.O.D.'s. Please allow up to 8 weeks for shipment.

Mr/Mrs/Miss _____

Address _____

City _____ State/Zip _____

Dell Bestsellers

- ☐ **SHOGUN** by James Clavell $3.50 (17800-2)
- ☐ **JUST ABOVE MY HEAD**
  by James Baldwin $3.50 (14777-8)
- ☐ **FIREBRAND'S WOMAN**
  by Vanessa Royall $2.95 (12597-9)
- ☐ **THE ESTABLISHMENT** by Howard Fast $3.25 (12296-1)
- ☐ **LOVING** by Danielle Steel $2.75 (14684-4)
- ☐ **THE TOP OF THE HILL** by Irwin Shaw $2.95 (18976-4)
- ☐ **JAILBIRD** by Kurt Vonnegut $3.25 (15447-2)
- ☐ **THE ENGLISH HEIRESS**
  by Roberta Gellis $2.50 (12141-8)
- ☐ **EFFIGIES** by William K. Wells $2.95 (12245-7)
- ☐ **FRENCHMAN'S MISTRESS**
  by Irene Michaels $2.75 (12545-6)
- ☐ **ALL WE KNOW OF HEAVEN**
  by Dore Mullen $2.50 (10178-6)
- ☐ **THE POWERS THAT BE**
  by David Halberstam $3.50 (16997-6)
- ☐ **THE LURE** by Felice Picano $2.75 (15081-7)
- ☐ **THE SETTLERS**
  by William Stuart Long $2.95 (15923-7)
- ☐ **CLASS REUNION** by Rona Jaffe $2.75 (11408-X)
- ☐ **TAI-PAN** by James Clavell $3.25 (18462-2)
- ☐ **KING RAT** by James Clavell $2.50 (14546-5)
- ☐ **RICH MAN, POOR MAN** by Irwin Shaw $2.95 (17424-4)
- ☐ **THE IMMIGRANTS** by Howard Fast $3.25 (14175-3)
- ☐ **TO LOVE AGAIN** by Danielle Steel $2.50 (18631-5)